TINSEL TEARS

Also by the author:

GUIDED
WASTED
MIDNIGHT SHERBET
DEAD FINE

This book may contain mature scenes,
including discussions of sexuality, homophobia,
terminal illness, and references to sex.

Suitable for older readers.

TINSEL TEARS

TINSEL TEARS

Copyright © 2023 by Emma J. Smith

The following novel is a work of fiction. Any resemblance to persons, living or dead, is a coincidence; all characters and settings are the product of the author's imagination.

ISBN – 9798866996797

All rights reserved. No part of these works can be reproduced, scanned, rewritten or translated in any form, digital or traditional, without the permission of the author.

emmasmithbooks.com

for all of the big kids who
never stopped believing in
the magic of Christmas…

PROLOGUE

"Mum? Dad?"

Abe turned his head from side to side, watching his parents carefully. It was Christmas Day, and the table lay set before them, the aftermath of a meal: a goose's carcass, flat on a platter, torn and shredded; a bowl of tatties, dripping in fat, now cold; the bread sauce growing a skin. Mr and Mrs Cane hadn't bought a turkey this year – "it's just so *dry*, and we only end up wasting the leftovers" – and so the goose gravy was watery and orange, set aside in their best ceramic boat.

Abe swallowed as Mrs Cane reached for the potatoes, picking two with a pair of tongs and placing them on her plate. There were four left, but Abe was too nervous to eat any more. He clutched the table's edge with trembling hands as his mother proceeded to quarter the potato before her, spearing it with a fork, little finger pointed outwards.

"What is it, dear?" she asked, glancing up to meet his gaze. "Did you enjoy your meal?"

Abe nodded, throat still dry. In an attempt to make sure his voice still worked, he reached for the eggnog and took a sip. *Come on, Abe. You can do this.*

He cleared his throat, turning back to his parents.

This was it. This was his moment…

"I need to tell you something."

Mr Cane picked up a sprout between his thumb and forefinger, examining it closely. "Isn't the humble sprout a *wonderful* thing? It's just so magical that we can now grow them here, in the North Pole! I remember the days when we did deals with British government, got them on the cheap... barrels of them, there were! Santa even had a warehouse built to store them in, at the end of town. Deary me. Those were the days!"

Abe coughed again. "Dad –"

"Of course, with modern technology nowadays, there's nothing we can't produce! It's wonderful, Mary, it really is..."

"Dad –"

"Oh, I know, Gerald, I do. I remember it well! And we couldn't get sprouts for the rest of the year, could we? Just at Christmas!"

"*Mum –*"

"And parsnips – why, I *do* love a parsnip – they had a four month availability slot, do you remember?"

"I'm gay."

Silence rippled across the table. Abe gulped, taking his finger and swiping it across the table. Dripping with gravy, he lifted it to his mouth to lick, desperate for *something* to occupy his shaking hands.

The slurping noise echoed around the room.

"You're... *gay?*" Mrs Cane asked, testing the word out in her mouth. She stared at her son in horror, eyes wide and unblinking. "Gay as in... you like *other boys?*"

"Yes, Mum," Abe said confidently, though his cheeks were flushed pink and he took another fingerful of gravy in haste. "I like... *other boys.*"

His parents looked to and from one another, still shocked,

mouths hung open. Mr Cane still had half a sprout on the end of his fork, which he dropped to his plate with a clatter, splattering juices from the goose and cranberry sauce across the table. Orangey-brown liquid formed a puddle on the white, and Abe could already imagine his mother's face as she tried to scrub the stain.

"But… you *can't* like boys," he objected, shaking his head madly. "Can he, Mary? You liked that lovely young elf back when you were still a nipper – oh, what was *her* name – and you've never shown an interest in haberdashery! Everyone knows what *their* tendencies are."

Abe's face was bright red now, and he stared down at his plate in embarrassment. The rumour about the elves in haberdashery was just that – a *rumour* – and the elf in question had seemed pretty enough when they were five years old and barely out of nappies.

He glanced up in time to see his mother dabbing a tissue against her eye, sniffing.

"Mum…" he began again, but she waved a hand in his direction.

"Don't, Abraham." She turned to Mr Cane in despair, tissue flapping and head rocking back and forth. "How *can* he be gay? Elves aren't gay! It's not right!"

"Don't stress yourself, Mary." Mr Cane consoled his wife, though he was staring at Abe with an expression of confusion. It was like he was trying to read a book in a language he didn't understand, and his brow wrinkled. "I mean, he might just be confused…"

"I'm not con–" his son tried to say, but Mrs Cane immediately cut in.

"Confused, of *course*, of course." She tipped her head back in order to breathe properly, tight curls wobbling. Abe had always jokingly thought his mother's hair resembled a stalk of sprouts, but he thought it now with a vengeance, curling his fists beneath the table.

"I think I heard about this on an American radio show, Gerald... they're in a right state over there. I blame drugs." Mrs Cane paused, saying delicately to her son, "Yes, that's right, darling. You're just confused. Maybe we should talk all of this through?"

"I'm *not* confused!" Abe repeated, but they weren't listening, they just weren't *listening*.

"And we'll still have grandchildren..." Mr Cane glanced worriedly around the room. "We'll still be able to continue the business, keep making shoes for disadvantaged kiddies... and if Abraham *does* transfer to haberdashery, only while he's figuring things out, we can quite easily take on another member of staff!"

It was no good. His parents weren't having any of it. Flushed stark vermillion, tips of his pointed ears tingling, Abe pushed back his chair and scowled at his parents.

"Merry Christmas," he spat, though he could feel tears welling behind his eyes and had to swallow them back for fear that they'd spill. *Drat, you darned emotions!* "You know, the one thing I wanted this year was for you to accept me..." His parents glanced at each other, eyes wide and expressions sheepish. "But I guess that was too much to ask."

He made his way to the door and pulled it open, turning back at the last minute to gaze at his father, who'd picked up the fork again and was examining the half-eaten sprout with pink cheeks.

"And Dad? Maybe I *will* go and work in haberdashery, if that's what you'd rather. I'll find a cute, equally *confused* elf to seduce, and once you've fully realised this *isn't* a phase and you definitely *won't be getting* any grandchildren, you can officially disown me."

"Abraham, that's hardly the way to –"

And then he slammed the door shut, right in their faces.

Merry Christmas, indeed.

Dear you...

I don't know who you are, but I know you're out there, somewhere. I think about how differently life must be for boys like you, and my chest aches. What must it be like to not have to hide, to shy away from the light? What must it be like to be free?

I know I'm not perfect, but I do try. I try to be brave, but something in me won't break free. I know what I'm meant to be and I know what I want, and I feel like my heart is breaking each time I try to work out... work out what I should do.

I want to be better, and I want to be bold. How can you... be so easily? How can you smile and laugh and live freely, when everyone is telling you to conform, conform, conform. I envy you in so many ways. All of you, with your glittered cheeks and ears pointed in pride, your boots and your smiles and your hearts on your sleeve, where they belong.

Sometimes, I fantasise about a place where I can be more like you. I fantasise about a world in which my parents want to learn, in which I'm brave enough to make them. I fantasise about you. I fantasise about kissing you, about touching you, about waking up in your shoes.

Sometimes, I even think my parents are right. Maybe I want to be you more than I want to be with you. Or maybe I simply want to adorn the bravery to be like you, in the hopes it might win me one of you.

A boy. That's all I want. Just a boy.

One who will love me and see my truth, see my honestly, my value. One who will make me feel seen. One who will befriend Mum and Dad, bring them round. One who will take me in his arms and declare me his, for all eternity.

I want you, but you're just a dream, aren't you? If you were real, this letter would be signed, stamped and sealed, maybe addressed to somewhere far off in the Jul Region, where the mountains are tall and frosty and the elves run free.

Maybe one day, you'll come true.

All my love,

           Abe x

PART ONE

*the north pole
december 1983*

ONE

Abe checked his watch for the six hundredth time, eying the big hand. Quarter past four. They were fifteen minutes early and the hall was still empty, benches waiting in silence, tinsel hanging from window to window. The fizz of a Christmas come too soon hung in the air.

"I knew we ought to have arrived at four..." he muttered, jiggling his leg up and down. There was no way he was mentally prepared for this – no way he could cope with the onslaught of elves about to toss themselves through the door, glittery-cheeked and jingling with joy, ripe for the picking... like summer fruits he'd never seen, confident, completely and utterly –

"Oh, *Abe*." Lottie jerked his arm away from him, rolling her eyes and placing a pointed ear on his shoulder. "Stop checking your blooming watch! It won't make them come faster. They'll be here soon!"

Abe leaned back away from his best friend, leg still jumping up and down, eyes wide. Lottie didn't seem to understand the importance of the situation, even as its instigator – and she *really* didn't understand how desperately he was trying not to wet himself.

"But I don't *want* them to be here soon, Lotts! Oh, why

did I let you drag me here in the first place?" Abe closed his eyes. This was silly. A terrible, terrible idea. He pushed his head against the wall, shaking it and frowning, heart racing beneath his chest.

It was quite possibly the most stupid thing he'd ever done.

"I dragged you here," Lottie continued, pulling his arm back and taking his hand, smiling, "because you're a closeted, twenty-year-old elf who's *never* had a boyfriend, never kissed anyone, and is *still* a massive virgin, if I can even say that." She cocked her head to one side, fixing him with a huge grin. "And I'm *hoping* this will persuade you to come out again, because none of my other methods seem to be working. Though it's still entirely up to you, of course. No pressure."

Abe groaned. He'd heard this too many times before.

He wanted to come out. That was probably true, because he knew it was either that or spend the rest of his life alone… but he couldn't. Two months after that dreaded Christmas, age thirteen and armed with a handful of baby hairs, two international pamphlets entitled "how to tell your parents you're gay!" and an awful lot of eggnog, he'd leapt back into the closet with a flying jump. He could still remember the look on his mum's face, his dad's frequent mentions of haberdashery. The thought still made his chest fume.

It had been seven years now. Seven long, painful years. His parents hadn't mentioned his coming out attempt again, but he knew they thought about it. They were already looking at apprentices for their business, convinced that Abe would leave them to join haberdashery – which was *just a sodding rumour*.

"I made a mistake," he told them, late in February, sat in front of the fire with a broken pair of trainers and a needle and thread. "I was confused – of *course* I'm not gay."

And now, aged twenty, nothing had changed. Which was exactly *why* he was here, apparently.

What better opportunity could there possibly be?

When the two of them first saw the flyer some time in November, outside the town hall, Lottie turned to him with shining brown eyes and her mouth agape.

"This is it, Abe!" she crowed, jabbing at the paper in her hand with one ecstatic finger. "It's a doll-making class. Doll-making for beginners, apparently! I don't want to stereotype – in fact, I'm not going to, I'm *not* – but *surely* we might have more luck at that than at the blooming matchmaking dinners your parents keep throwing?"

Apparently it was fair game for Lottie to assume, because at that precise moment, an elf sidled up to them, all green trousers and bell-adorned shoes, sporting an upwards-twirled moustache and tiny glasses. Elves were more flamboyant than the humans he'd seen in films and on magazine covers, but they were also creatures of tradition. Abe hadn't seen an upwards-twirled moustache since his last trip to the American Cinema at the bottom of Tinsel Street.

"Do I sign up here?" he asked, turning to Abe.

Abe flushed and nodded, breathless, unable to speak. Rolling her eyes, Lottie pushed the sheet forward and smiled at the elf. "Yeah. You sign at the bottom."

The elf smirked at Abe, turning his face an even deeper shade of plum, pointed ears tingling. He signed his name with a flourish, before turning to Lottie and asking, "Do you think it'd be okay if I took this for my friends to sign? They'd find this pretty fun!"

"Sure!" Lottie said brightly, nodding her head. "No problem! See you there!"

"Yeah…" The elf smiled, eyes flitting to Abe. "I'm Devlin,

by the way. I'll be seeing you both!"

It had been almost three weeks, now. Here they were, sat on a hard bench at the edge of the hall, staring round at the empty room and waiting for it to fill with ridiculously cool elves like Devlin, elves who most likely had it all figured out, elves who were calm, collected, fine with being who they were. Maybe even elves whose parents weren't ridiculously traditional, who didn't want to learn... elves who weren't forced to *hide*.

These were elves with *experience*. Not only had they kissed other elves, but they probably weren't still virgins like him and Lottie. And most importantly, they had experience with other *male* elves, which was exactly what Abe wanted most.

"I can't do this," he said suddenly, turning to Lottie and shaking his head. "I don't know how to talk to boys – I don't even know how to act around *girls* half the time!" He stood up, hands trembling, and balled them into fists by his sides. "I don't even *want* to come out, Lottie. This is all you! I'd rather just stay in the closet forever."

She rolled her eyes and tried to grab his arm to force him back down, but he jerked it away. With that, he stomped from the room, crossing the threshold and slamming straight into –

"Ow!"

Abe collided with the snow-ridden pavement, face first, arms and limbs flailing. Ice filled his mouth and slid over his tongue as he choked, turning over into a soft, grey pillow...

"What the..."

He scrambled up, eyes wide staring down at the elf below him.

"I'm *so* sorry, I didn't mean to –" Abe stopped, heart racing, and took a step backwards. His cheeks were pink and his hands were still trembling.

And there, lying on the pavement, melting the snow beneath him, was the most beautiful boy he'd ever seen.

Oh my baubles, oh my baubles, oh my baubles –

"That wasn't deliberate, I'm honestly so sorry, I didn't mean to walk into you... or fall on top of you, I just –" He was tripping over his words in an attempt to apologise, staring with wide eyes at the boy, who seemed, if he wasn't mistaken, to be gazing *right back at him*.

"It's okay." The elf was smiling, amused, nose red with cold and eyelashes flecked with snow. He lay against the white like a grey marshmallow, stomach rounded and soft beneath a hoody and unzipped coat, the fluff of his hood like a soft mane. Abe could feel his mouth watering and hastily licked his lips, unable to tear his eyes from the elf's own. They were huge and liquid brown, like hot chocolate.

Abe *loved* hot chocolate.

"I'm Patrick."

"I'm..." But Abe could barely get his words out. Fumbling awkwardly, he held out a hand to Patrick and attempted to pull him up. His fingers were warm, oozy, like cookies on Christmas Eve.

"Hi." Patrick was stood in front of him, inches away from his face, smiling shyly.

Abe swallowed.

"Hello." He took another deep breath, then managed, "I'm Abe."

"Abe?" Patrick cocked his head to one side, then grinned. "Short for Abraham?"

Abe nodded. He could feel all of the phlegm in his body rising up his throat, and swallowed.

"Cool name!" Patrick responded. "Means father, or

something like that, right?"

"It does?" Abe replied. He was unsure of whether he was agreeing or questioning, and Patrick giggled. His parents had seen the name in a magazine or something, before he was born; it wasn't the fanciest of origin stories. If it really did mean father, that was ironic, seeing as he didn't think he'd ever *be* one.

But the boys stared at each other for a moment longer, quiet hanging thickly in the air, the crackle of sparks alight between them.

The silence was broken by the sound of footsteps on the snow behind them, the burbling of laughter, a snowball being thrown at the wall, exploding out into the crisp air.

Abe swivelled and sucked in a breath.

Devlin was striding towards them, all bell-adorned boots and big smile, eyebrows perfectly tamed and moustache swizzled, flanked by an army of other guys. They were toned and tall, dressed in well-fitting clothes with high-brand labels, the kind imported from England or America or Italy, items they'd never, ever make in the North Pole.

Devlin raised a hand to greet him before they slipped inside the town hall like shadows, leaving behind a trail of mystery and awe.

He hadn't recognised Abe. Of *course* he hadn't.

"We should…" Abe gestured to the door while Patrick shook himself, removing the leftover snow, and nodded in agreement.

"Yeah."

They stood there for another moment, looking at each other awkwardly, before Abe repeated, "Yeah." He took a step towards the door, nodding, cheeks still burning.

"It was nice meeting you," he said, attempting a smile.

"I'm sorry about earlier – I really didn't mean to collide with you."

"It's fine." Patrick smiled back.

And then he walked past him, giving his shoulder a gentle tap, and disappeared into the hall.

For a moment, Abe just stood there. A light breeze tickled his face, promising a fresh flurry of snow, yet he couldn't bring himself to *move*.

Had that interaction been real? Had Patrick, with his snow-flecked lashes and cookie dough fingers, really just stood before him and held his hands like that, as though he was a bird about to take flight? Or had he been a vision, an angel formed from stardust, perfection at its finest?

"Am I dreaming?" he asked out loud, and jumped as the sound met his ears. Goodness. So Patrick really *was* real.

The hall was full when he found his way inside, packed with elves who filled each bench, fizzing with laughter and nodding around at the hubbub. The lights were on, casting a warm glow on the decorations, which seemed to have been given a fresh burst of festive spirit; no doubt someone had sprinkled magic across the tinsel and sagging gold stars, lifting them higher into the boughs of the roof, where they lit the space. Abe made his way over to Lottie with his hands tucked firmly beneath his sleeves, head ducked, and dropped onto the seat beside her.

"Where've you *been*?" she burst, staring at him with pink cheeks and wide eyes, an expression of fury across her face. "I thought you'd ditched me here, Abe! And for your information, I was quite looking forward to learning how to make dolls. This was supposed to be our thing!"

But Abe just shook his head, still shellshocked. "Lotts, I'm sorry, but –"

"But what? I was freaking out, Abe!"

"I met a boy."

Abe hesitated for a second, watching her expression change from angry to horrified, then from horrified to ecstatic, mouth curving into a grin.

"You did *what*?"

"I met a boy," Abe repeated, though he couldn't stop the smile from creeping onto his face this time. "A boy named… Patrick."

Lottie opened and closed her mouth, gobsmacked, whilst they stared at each other. Abe couldn't help his cheeks colouring, once again; he really, really wished he didn't blush so easily. But was it really so ludicrous that he should meet a boy? That was the whole reason they'd even *come* to the stupid doll-making class, after all.

As Lottie started to speak, silence fell in the hall. The class had begun. Abe picked up the two felt pieces on the desk before him and held them up, frowning, trying to figure out how on earth they combined to make a doll, creasing his brow in concentration.

Doll-making was *nothing* like fixing shoes.

As the instructor passed around ribbons and pompoms and faux fur, they got to work, fiddling and patching and threading.

"Detail last, remember. Get the basic shapes down first!"

"And I thought they were going to *teach* us something," Lottie whispered, nudging Abe under the table and rolling her eyes. "It's like the arts and crafts your mum would make us do, round at yours – do you remember?" She wrinkled her nose at his concentration. "So, come on! Tell me all about this Patrick!"

"Mhmm…" Abe nodded, concentrating hard on trying to

thread the needle in his hand. He cursed violently as it fell to the floor, bouncing under the next table, lost amid the racket. "Oh, golly, Lotts, I better go get that…"

Dropping to his knees, he disappeared under the tablecloth, letting it swallow him whole. The table was long and spanned the width of the hall, flanked by benches, which were filled with elves. He crawled around sprawled legs and felted mules, scanning the floor desperately for a pinprick of silver.

"Oh, please," he whispered, patting his fingers against the floorboards. "Where are you…"

Light flooded under the table all of a sudden, spilling over Abe. He blinked upwards, eyes meeting deep, chocolate brown, and –

"Oh," a voice said softly, almost inaudible above the hall's chatter. "It's you."

Dear Abraham Cane,

If this isn't Abraham Cane, sod off and reseal the envelope!

Hi, Abe! I got your address from the sign-up sheet - I know that sounds creepy, but I hope you don't mind! You seemed so eager to apologise for knocking me down, but it's honestly fine... I should have looked where I was going, ha-ha! I'm always knocking into things. Mum says I'm like a walking bauble, all bouncy - with luckily soft edges!

Anyway, I was wondering if you wanted to maybe go for a hot chocolate some time, get some food? I work at the café on Tinsel Street (the Wonky Angel, to the end, by the dustbins), and I'm free every night at seven, which is when my shift ends. If you're interested, just drop by and we'll go out somewhere!

Merry Christmas, Abe!

Lots of love and sprinkles,
      Patrick xxx

TWO

It was December second, and Abe was sat on his bed, sifting through envelopes and cards. The Christmas post started rolling in around mid-November, and he already had a string of cards lined across the fireplace, reaching towards the open flames.

He tore at them in dissatisfaction as snow fell outside his window. His apartment was illuminated in the dark night by a perfect full moon, which lay opposite, smothered in a bed of trees. It was cold – very cold.

Pulling his dressing gown further around him, Abe frowned and turned the next envelope upside down, so he could read it properly, brow creasing as he tried to recognise the postmark.

"The Natale Region..." he muttered, pushing a finger under the flap to pull it open. "Why on earth would..."

A card fell onto his lap, small and square, undeserving of the large, rectangular envelope. It was mismatched and faded, almost like someone had tried to formulate a gift card from items at the bottom of their cupboard. The Natale Region was known for being the poorest part of the North Pole; most of the elves there worked in the larger toy factories, ones which made tacky, plastic products, the kind sweeping the globe in a frenzy. The work there wasn't great – or well-paid.

Abe had never even *spoken* to an elf from that part of the North Pole... not that he could remember. His father mended shoes for disadvantaged children, a bespoke craft the family had long perfected by hand, and he'd grown up in a circle of high-standing elves. Elves who had money, traditional values, high status. Elves who were closer to Santa himself, and got pretty cream invites to his yearly ball.

So why had he received a card from the Natale Region?

With curious fingers, he thumbed open the card, pulling it out onto the duvet.

His heart stopped.

It couldn't be. Abe's eyes had skipped straight to the bottom of the page, where, in neat block capitals, read Patrick's name.

Patrick.

Patrick.

Abe just stared at the card for a moment, mouth a perfect "o" shape.

Dear Abraham Cane...

Was this even real?

It couldn't be.

Things like this just didn't *happen* to him.

Or... did they?

Had his luck finally started to change?

And Patrick... Patrick thought he was weird. After he crawled under his bench and appeared to be rummaging around his feet, Abe promptly flushed a horrendous shade of red and rushed back to his own seat, without uttering a word. After such bizarre behaviour, Abe had vowed never to return to the doll-making class again, to hibernate deep inside his closet for the rest of his existence.

But… now *this*.

He read the page over and over, eyes skimming the cheap writing and kiss – one kiss, not two or three – and taking in every nick and smudge, every dot of ink, flick of a letter, rounded vowel.

He'd been asked on a date. A real-life *date*. Given that he wasn't joking, of course – that was always a possibility.

But a *date*. A date with food, fairy lights, maybe some tender hand-touching… and whatever else people did on dates. He didn't know; he'd never actually *been* on one.

Yet here he was, about to meet Patrick, the beautiful brown-eyed boy, the boy with snow-flecked lashes and a smile like warmed honey, on *Tinsel Street*, of all places, a street full of cobbles and tiny shops and overhanging buildings, built all crooked to make the most of the sky…

"Oh my baubles," he whispered, leaning back against his pillow with a blissful smile on his face. "Wait until I tell Lottie…"

***

Tinsel Street was all lit up with lights as Abe made his way to the café, hands in his pockets and heart racing. It really was beautiful here, all warm and festive, like a Christmassy hug. It made total sense that Patrick would work in a place like this. The streets were lined with old stone cobbles, windows arched with black and gold, lights hung from every rooftop in all shades of warmth.

"Would you like to buy a cookie, young man?" one vendor shouted, from behind his table. An array of biscuits and treats lay before him on soft white tissue paper, like snow. "One for you, or one for your lady friend!"

But Abe just blushed, shaking his head and wafting a hand in the man's direction. He could buy one each for him and Patrick, only he wasn't planning on actually *seeing* Patrick tonight. He needed to stake out the situation first.

The sky was dark as he wandered further, surrounded by candles and tinsel, trees and fur trims, jangling bells and crying vendors. Carollers at one corner burst with song as he passed, and he dropped a lolly into their collection bucket, just to be jovial, just as an older couple passed him and smiled, crying their merry Christmases and docking their pointed caps in his direction.

It was impossible *not* to love Christmas at the North Pole.

The café was right at the bottom of Tinsel Street, tucked away beneath a rickety, overhanging building, painted white between beams of black wood. It wasn't the kind of place you could subtly stare into without being noticed, so Abe cowered around the edge of the next building, watching with narrowed eyes.

And there, in the window, was Patrick.

He was wearing a grey hoodie, faded and worn, beneath a navy apron which tied around his stomach like a scarf. He was smiling, too, lifting a plate of chocolate cupcakes onto a table and opening his mouth to say something. Abe tried to read his lips, realising too late that that was entirely the wrong body part to be focusing on and flushing promptly.

How on earth was Patrick so blooming *cute*?

With a thumping heart and trembling hands, Abe pulled himself forwards along the wall, towards the café's window –

"Excuse me?"

Abe jumped, spinning round as a voice sounded from behind him.

"Can I help you?"

It was a boy, stood before him in that same navy apron and a pair of saggy chinos. He was clutching a bag of rubbish to his chest and frowning at him, eyebrows knitted.

Abe felt his throat run dry and licked his lips nervously. Clearing his throat, he muttered, "No, sorry, I was just –"

"Watching Pat through the window?" The boy raised his eyes, unimpressed, and flicked his wrist in the direction of the café. "Sorry to assume, but you're acting exactly like the last five boys he invited to linger. Lovestruck eyes, flushed cheeks, *super* ugly shoes…" His eyes moved down to Abe's felted mules, an amused smile on his lips. "Get over it, bud. It's pretty pathetic."

He moved over to the bin, tipping the bag up and emptying a mound of rubbish.

Abe stood still for a moment, wringing his hands in front of him. A cold breeze blew down the street and through his hair; shoppers wandered leisurely past him on their way home, with no notion of what was going on beside them, what internal pain was gripping Abe as he swayed on his feet, shellshocked, eyes fixed to the bin.

"There's no point denying it," the boy continued, even though Abe was doing nothing of the sort. "Like I said, I've seen it time and time again. You're lucky I got to you first."

Abe nodded. There was no doubt he was crestfallen – that was apparent just from his face – and yet he wasn't quite sure *why*. Had he ever really believed he had a chance with Patrick?

"I… I'm just here to check the prices of…" He glanced up at the menu on the wall, written in pink and red on a rickety chalkboard. "I'm checking the prices of the hot chocolates." He swallowed, glancing back at the boy, who was now staring back with one eyebrow raised. "I was thinking of taking my girlfriend here…"

"Poor girl." The boy let out a snort of laughter, then picked up his now empty bags and swung them over his shoulder. "See you, bud. Good luck next time, yeah?"

Abe watched as he disappeared back inside the café. It had been stupid to even come here in the first place. A ridiculous idea, bound to bring him hurt and trouble. He should've just stayed firmly in the closet, where he belonged.

He started to walk away as tears welled in his eyes, and brushed them away rapidly. *Damn* him for crying in front of him. Would he never learn?

"Abe!"

He stopped walking, heart pounding in his eardrums. Had someone just shouted his name, or was he... imagining things? He almost didn't want to find out. He'd had enough disappointment for one day.

But slowly, one foot after the other, he turned around.

There, stood before him in his navy apron with his hair all mussed-up and a huge smile on his face, was Patrick.

"Uh-h..." Abe stuttered, flushed red. He stared back at him for a moment, before forcing out a, "Hello."

"You came!" Patrick strode forward, still beaming, and held open his arms. "David said you wouldn't, but I had faith in you. It's so good to see you!"

Still blushing furiously, Abe stepped forwards into Patrick's arms, and... *oh*. It was like he'd been enveloped in the arms of a great brown teddy bear, all warm paws and fusty, cosy scent, plush stomach soft against his own, messy hair against his cheek. He swallowed nervously as he stepped back into the cold, gazing back at Patrick's chocolate eyes. Then he remembered what the boy had said earlier, and everything came back with a crash.

You're acting exactly like the last five boys he invited to linger…

He was just so blooming pathetic.

"I was just passing," he said quickly, twisting to leave. "Just… checking the hot chocolate prices, you know."

Patrick cocked his head to one side, then rolled his eyes and tipped back his head to laugh. It was a rich, tinkly laugh, one which sent shivers down Abe's spine.

"You spoke to David, didn't you?" Patrick noted the confusion on his face, and added, "The other waiter? My best friend, David – he's a bit protective over me. I told him about you, and I think he just wanted to suss you out, check you didn't have bad intentions."

"I don't!" Abe burst, then flushed again, this time a bright, furious red. "I mean… I'm just here to check the prices, like I said."

"So you *don't* want to go out with me?" Patrick grinned, teasing.

Abraham shivered. "I… I never said that."

They just stared at each other again, for another moment, two hearts beating in sync.

"My shift finishes at seven." Patrick's voice was low, throaty, amid the hustle and bustle of shoppers. A line of electricity, slow and tentative, zipped between them, spluttering sparks and nervous energy.

"I have nothing on tonight…" Abe gulped, twisting his hands round and round in circles, then offered up a smile. "I can hang around here for a bit, if you'd like?"

"That sounds perfect." Patrick was beaming properly now, teeth on show, cheeks pink and shining. "Or… I could, I don't know, *actually* buy you a hot chocolate?"

"It's a deal."

Dear Patrick,

I'd love to come to your cafe, if that's still okay with you. I'm not free on the suggested date, but will the options on the back of his letter suit you? If you return to sender, I can mark it into my diary.

It was lovely meeting you the other night, too. You seem like a lovely boy, and I really would like to get to know you better. You didn't seem too offended by my bumping into you, so that's a good thing, hey?

All my love,

    Abe x

F.Y.I: I don't think you look like a bauble at all, and I'm not sure whether your mum meant it endearingly or not. If it's any consolation, I've been referred to as a candy cane my whole life – note the surname, and my beanpole legs. People are cruel.

THREE

As snow fell against the window, it was warm inside the café. Candles hung from the walls in red and white holders, and an oil lamp swayed from side to side in the centre of the room, casting its surroundings in warm gold light.

Abe sat in the corner on a rickety table, nursing a steaming hot chocolate before him. Patrick had smothered it in extra cream and pink marshmallows, and a candy cane hung over the edge, releasing minty goodness into the vat.

He inhaled deeply, a smile laced across his face, and took a sip from the mug.

Ahh. Even the hot chocolate was perfect.

"Are you enjoying that?" A hopeful voice came from beside him, lilting, smiling. Abe turned, heartrate picking up, to find Patrick wiping down a table and watching eagerly for his reaction.

"It's delicious," Abe replied, cheeks flushed pink – because it was. Yet at this point, Patrick could've served him snails and frog legs, like he'd seen them do on French television, and Abe still would've eaten up the whole plate.

As seven ticked by, Abe was ready and waiting by the door. He was trembling, half from nerves and half from excitement. This was his *first ever date*, and despite knowing it would all be fine, he couldn't help but feel a little apprehensive. How many boys had Patrick dated before? Was he a virgin too? Would Abe's lack of experience put him off? The same questions whirred around his mind as he tapped his finger against the wall, faster and faster…

"Ready?" Patrick appeared beside him, apron removed and hooded coat on, teddy-bear stomach buttoned beneath. "Let's get ready to see the real Tinsel Street, Abraham!"

The door swung open, and they stepped outside.

The street was quieter now, colder, the chill rushing between their legs like water. Fog curled around lampposts and piles of slush gathered on the pavements and between cobbles, trampled by passers-by into grey-brown clumps. Above them, however, was a clear sky, inky blue and stretched like a canvas; it was interrupted only by pinpricks of light, shining through in the shape of tiny silver stars.

Abe sighed, tilting his head up to stare at the sky above, and was caught off guard by a warm hand reaching for his.

"The North Pole is like a whole other world at night," Patrick said, smiling. "Come on, Abraham. I want to show you where the fun is *really* at!"

The street swivelled suddenly as Abe felt himself being tugged down an alleyway, away from the lights and bright smiles and into darkness. Cobbles fell away to snow-covered dirt and he placed his feet purposefully so as not to slip over, clutching Patrick's fingers to keep himself standing.

"Where are we going?" he wondered out loud, but Patrick simply let out a tinkly laugh, stepping up the pace.

The alley broke into a clearing a few metres away, and so they jogged the last few steps, shoes crunching on the untrodden snow. A blanket of white unfurled before them, a carpet of promise and freedom, untouched, ready for them to make their mark.

"It's just a little further," Patrick murmured, squeezing Abe's hand and grinning at him beneath the moonlight. "Just down here…"

Their shoes made footprints in the snow, the pattern of two boys wandering hand in hand, in sync. Smokey-breathed and bright eyed, Patrick tugged him across the snow, surrounded by trees and the dark night's sky, closer and closer to a bauble of light, just visible through a copse of trees.

Abe's hand left Patrick's as he reached to push through the branches.

"What the…" he murmured.

Then he stopped.

There, in front of them, towering up into the evening sky, was a tunnel of light. It cascaded stars and snowflakes and glistening candles in a mess of magical light, arching above them to meet in the middle like two hands, touching fingertips for the first time and bursting into sparks.

"I…" Abe tried to say, but the words got caught in his mouth and he spluttered breathlessly, gazing up at the roof of the cave with wide blue eyes.

"Come on," Patrick said, grinning and taking his hand again. Palm to palm, fingers intertwined, they made their way into the light.

"How did you even know this place *existed*?" Abe asked in wonder, though he couldn't look at Patrick. He was too in awe of his surroundings, reaching up to touch the lights and beaming as his fingers fizzed with the magic of it all. "It's so… beautiful."

"My ex works just down here… you'll see soon enough." He beamed in Abe's direction, meeting his eye. "It's crazy, I promise you. She's a waitress. I love my job, obviously, but hers takes the biscuit."

"She?" Abe echoed, expression faltering. But before he could extract his hand, Patrick burst out laughing, shaking his head.

"Sorry, I didn't really explain that too well, did I?" He smiled at Abe's confusion, squeezing tight. "I'm bisexual. Don't worry. You didn't get the wrong impression."

"You're…" Abe nodded, relief flooding through his body. "Oh. Oh, okay." He paused, trying to muster the courage to say what he wanted to, for only the third time in his life. "I'm… I'm gay."

"Okay," Patrick said, eyeing him with an interested smile. "Cool. Thank you for telling me, Abe."

And although Abe couldn't tell what Patrick was feeling, something inside him swelled with pride.

The path took a turn then, curving sidewards as the arch twisted left, tunnel widening. Their footsteps were silent, the ground slick with wet mud and dregs of snow. There was no need to say anything else. Abe's heart was racing as they wandered leisurely, not wanting to rush things, to miss *anything* out. Each light, each tiny bulb, each flickering flame held by its magical sphere…

"There it is!" Patrick exclaimed suddenly, lifting a hand to point. "Welcome to the Gingerbread Restaurant, Abraham!"

And there, right in front of them, was a real-life gingerbread house.

"You mean…"

"It's made of gingerbread, yes!" Patrick grinned, giving a tiny leap to express his joy. "It's exactly like the ones they make in bakeries, only bigger and better. You *can* eat it, but I wouldn't recommend it. The outside layer is always so cold!"

They paced forwards, faster now, towards the chocolate

door. It loomed above them in all its two-floor glory; windows of candy shone with light, and a chocolate door read "open" in black icing letters, the doorknob studded with tiny, crystallised candy cane pieces. To test it out, Abe reached to pluck a green gummy from the brick exterior, and no sooner had he placed it on his tongue had it grown back again, emerging from the gingerbread like a little lime wart.

"This is amazing," he murmured, eyes wide. "I can't believe I never knew about it!"

"It's kind of prestigious," Patrick explained, hovering with his hand above the knob. "That's why it's so expensive. But I get a discount, so we're good."

Abe nodded, remembering Patrick's letter from the Natale Region. He probably wasn't rolling in cash.

"My ex – Dora – is more like a best friend to me." Patrick breathed in deeply, pulling a sheepish face. "We shouldn't have dated, but we were eighteen and dumb, and we risked our entire friendship. I… I thought I should let you know. Please don't think it's weird for me to bring you here, or anything like that."

"I get it," Abe replied, though he didn't really. He'd never done anything of the sort. Imagining dating Lottie made him *deeply* uncomfortable, even if his parents had always hinted that they'd quite approve. Her parents moved in their circles, and the six of them often had dinner parties together or took trips out of Noël.

"Dora and David are a little protective over me, but she *really* wants to meet you." Patrick grinned, letting go of his hand and smiling reassuringly. "I promise, Abe."

And with that, he pushed open the door.

The scent of chocolate was instant, and Abe breathed in deeply as it hit him, wafting in waves of warm cocoa. They stepped through the doorway and into the Gingerbread Restaurant, one step, two step, tentative. Abe's heartrate slowed.

It was like walking into a dream.

The room was vast, stretching out across a fudgy carpet and into a wide dining area, surrounded by orangey gingerbread bricks which decorated the walls. Huge windows reached to the ceiling and shone in the candlelight, dented and imperfect, smelted with sugary goodness. Each sill was carved from elaborate marzipan, marbled with pink and white, and spun sugar curtains hung from a nougat rod.

"Let's go to the back," Patrick said, gesturing sidewards. "It's always a little busy around Christmas, but we must've caught a quiet day…"

Elves perched on tables around the room; they sat on platforms set high on the wall, or on the first floor, which peeked over them from a balcony high above. An elderly couple with pointed ears peering from beneath their grey curls smiled and lifted papery hands to wave at them, and Abe shivered, immediately taking a step away from Patrick, just in case he was standing too close. It was instinctive, the rush to defend his secret.

"Are you okay?" Patrick asked, frowning. "Come on. You've got to try the food here, Abe. It's insane!"

They found a table at the very back of the room, by a large window, overlooking the snowy plains below. A fresh storm was brewing and flakes of white danced down from the sky above, and as Patrick pulled out a chair for him to sit down on, giving a tiny flick of his hand, Abe couldn't help but smile. He wasn't sure if this was even *real*. How could it be? The restaurant – or the gingerbread house – and the fields beyond, stretching out like a shiny white lake, all seemed straight out of an illustration, the perfect image of Christmas at the North Pole...

"Okay!" Patrick settled opposite him, reaching for the menu between them. "You've got to try the millionaire's shortbread; that's a must. And the turkey sandwich... I might order a bit of everything. I can't decide what *not* to get!"

"I don't mind." Abe flushed, rubbing the back of his neck. He didn't know what else to say – or to *do*, even. He sat there, terrified, as Patrick's eyes ran over the menu before him to pick out their orders.

"Sorted," he said, eyes lighting up as he prodded the page eagerly. "I've got it! The sharing platter, for our starter, main and dessert. A bit of everything!" He glanced up, face falling as he noted Abe's pink cheeks and awkward hand hovering behind his head. "I'm sorry, I'm taking over, aren't I? My friends say I do that when I'm nervous. I talk too much. Dora and David are so quiet, I'm used to filling the silences."

"Oh, don't apologise!" Abe leaned forward, shaking his head, despite his quivering insides. "I just... I've never been on a date before, see. And... I'm not out yet, so..."

"So... this *is* a date, then?"

Abe opened his mouth to protest, every inch of his face turning red... until he noticed Patrick smirking, and sank back into his chair, even more embarrassed.

"I'm glad we're on the same page, Abraham." Patrick placed the menu down and glanced up with pink cheeks. "I've never actually been on a date with a boy, see. Only ever with Dora, and we were friends first, so... if I make a fool of myself, I apologise in advance."

"You're doing great so far," Abe replied, coughing and looking away. "So... shall we order?"

Dear Abe,

You'll receive this letter after our date (because you'd best believe I wrote this on a bathroom break, on a piece of loo roll - sorry, not sorry) but I couldn't not write down how I'm feeling about this, about you, about all of this. Part of me wants to explode into fireworks, but another part wants to hold you tight, in my hand. Careful, though, because this all feels so fragile and I don't want to break it.

I've never felt this way before, that's for sure. No boy - or girl - has ever felt so... me. It's easy with you. The talking, the laughter, the spark. You make me want to explore myself, as well as you. You make me feel alive.

I know this is scary for you, that you're still closeted and scared to tell the world, but I know what that feels like, and I'm here for you. We can go at our own pace. I just want to see where this can go, you know? I want to learn more about you. I want to learn everything about you.

Lots of love and sprinkles,
        Patrick xxx

FOUR

Abe had never actually drunk before. A glass of mulled wine every so often during the winter months, maybe, and the occasional tipple on New Year's Eve… but as Dora pushed the cocktail across the table towards him, he couldn't help but salivate.

"It's mince pie flavour!" she gushed, smiling giddily. She was a tiny elf, with skinny wrists and ankles, and cheekbones which stood out against her pale skin. She hardly said a word as they ordered, but as soon as the food arrived, arms buckling under the trays, she couldn't stop talking. "Doesn't it look *insane*, Abe?"

"What's in it?" he asked. Taking the glass in his hands, he examined the sugar-encrusted rim and a floating dried orange, saturated in something glittery and gold.

"It's mainly grape and cranberry juice," she explained. "With a cherry liqueur and a dash of brandy, orange extract, a cinnamon syrup from one of the stores in town, made locally! Try it!"

Abe lifted the glass to his lips, feeling the sweetness against his tongue. It tasted exactly like a cold mince pie, fresh from the fridge, buttery pastry and all.

"It's lovely," he said, smiling back. "Really lovely!"

The starters came next, on platters of silver, placed in the centre of the table next to the candle. Tiny slices of bread, almost like crackers, with Wensleydale and slivers of smoked salmon; delicate prawn cocktail in crystal shot glasses; mozzarella sticks, wrapped in crispy breadcrumbs; pigs in blankets, still hot from the oven; individual mugs of roasted beetroot soup, with dinky croutons.

"Good job I have a big appetite!" Patrick said, grinning and lifting a mozzarella stick to his lips as he smacked his belly. "This food is too good!"

Whether it was the alcohol or the company, he didn't know… Abe began to laugh. It was the first genuine sound to leave his mouth since meeting Patrick, the first noise which was *natural*, not awkward or shy. It was just a laugh.

They gorged on turkey and stuffing sandwiches for their main course, with soft, gravy-soaked bread, cranberry sauce, slices of sage and onion stuffing, and lashings of red cabbage shredded across the carnage. A plate of crispy roast potatoes with plenty of rosemary finished off the table, and two pots of steaming nutmeg tea sat by their fingers, smiling up at them.

Abe had gravy all round his mouth, dribbling down his chin. Patrick reached up to wipe it away with a smile, and Abe felt himself flushing at the feel of foreign fingers grazing his jaw, the corner of his mouth…

And they talked. They talked and talked, right through all of the food, until they ran out of generic questions and switched to the deeper stuff, diving beneath each other to query their lives, their beliefs, their thoughts, their ideas. Abe learnt that Patrick was twenty-one, liked Mexican fried chicken and the colour blue, and was a huge Justin Bieber fan; Patrick learnt that Abe was twenty, working at his parents' shop, couldn't stand spicy food, and was hoping to take over the shoe shop one day, follow in the Cane family footsteps.

"Why?" Patrick asked curiously. "I'm not judging. I genuinely want to know."

"I... I don't know." Because that was the honest answer. Abe really *didn't* know. It'd always just been a given, an offer too good to ignore. He was to make shoes for underprivileged children, taking over the company from his father, and make a substantial amount of money to save for retirement, which was when he'd pass it over to *his* children.

If he had any, that was.

"What's your passion, then?" Patrick pressed. "Is it the shoe thing? You know, making disadvantaged children happy at Christmas, and all that?"

Abe shrugged. "I mean, that means a lot to me, of course – it would mean a lot to anyone – but I'm not super excited about waking up and fixing shoes every day, not like my dad is. He loves it. The business, the house, everything. It's his whole life." He glanced down at the table, ears turned pink once again. "That's why he was so crushed when I tried to come out to them both, seven Christmases ago. He... well, he wants me to carry on the business, give it to my kids, you know."

Patrick nodded, cocking his head to one side. "Yeah. I get it. It's unlucky. My mum's pretty accepting, but then... she's got a lot on her plate, you know? Five kids, hardly any money. The fact that I'm bi is the least of her worries. She just wants me to be happy."

"What about your dad?" Abe asked. "Does he approve?"

"My dad... well, he's not exactly on the scene anymore." Patrick took a bite of his turkey sandwich and bit down, hard, chewing just to fill the silence. "He left when I was twelve. He was sleeping with one of the factory managers. Mum worked nights and slept during the day, so he'd bring her back during their lunch break and do it in my little brother's bed. We found a used condom while we were playing in there one day, and the poor kid thought it was the wrapper for a cinnamon chew, got all excited. Mum kicked him out that evening."

Abe just stared at him for a moment, trying to take it in.

He couldn't imagine his parents, the dedicated and devoted Gerald and Mary Cane, *ever* cheating on each other. They'd never so much as fallen out in front of him before, even had a tiff. It wasn't as it either of them would win a prize for being desirable to singletons, either. Mrs Cane's wrinkled neck and her husband's shrivelled legs indicated a forgotten sell-by date… just two prunes, left to disintegrate on the back of a shelf.

"So yeah." Patrick let out a grim laugh, brown eyes focused on his plate. "He probably would've hated the fact I'm bisexual, so I'm not missing out on much. He was awful, a total narcissist. He screwed my mum over, and I'll never forgive him for that."

Although he was shaking and his mouth was dry, Abe reached out across the table to clasp his hand. Their fingers twisted into place and Patrick looked up to smile at him, meeting his gaze in a collision of brown against blue.

Oh my baubles, oh my baubles, oh my baubles –

Dessert arrived well on into the evening, served on tiny white dishes with silver forks. A rich mousse of white chocolate, garnished with mint; cardamom ice cream and delicate shortbread biscuits; festive millionaire's shortbread, the caramel laced with glacé cherries; iced mince pies, sugary and buttery and full of melt-in-your-mouth goodness.

And more cocktails, of course. Cocktails filled with

amaretto and white chocolate liqueur, and strawberry and cherry syrup, covered in crystallised fruit slices and mounds of glitter.

"This is incredible," Abe said, through a mouthful of mousse. "I don't think I've eaten such good food in all my life…"

"You should try the summer menu," Patrick replied, beaming. "Their strawberry spiced latte is to *die* for, Abe. I'll buy you one, when the time comes."

To that, Abe glanced down at the table with a hideous grin stretched across his face. Summer implied that they'd still be dating by then; that their relationship, or whatever it currently was, would last the coming year. Despite the fact they'd only known each other one night, Abe couldn't help but feel good about this – about Patrick. Although he'd never dated anyone before, not even a little bit, something about Patrick just felt so… right. It felt safe. As the room slowly emptied and the snowstorm flurried outside in a whirlwind of white, they were locked in a bubble of happiness, unable to stop talking, the smiles on their faces locked safely into place.

They left around midnight, creeping out into the night with linked hands and held breaths, bodies lapsed in silence. Wandering through the tunnel of lights, shoes squelching over the wet ground, it was as though they were trapped in the most perfect of dreams, locked and sealed into place.

Tinsel Street was near empty, the shop fronts closed, lights hung across in a smiley zigzag.

"I'll walk you home," Patrick offered hopefully. "Where did you say you lived?"

"I have a flat down in the Noël Region," Abe replied. "You don't have to walk me though, I'll be fine by myself…"

Patrick grinned and squeezed his hand in a silent promise.

The Noël Region was part of the richer side of town, where houses leaned over the moonlit river with lavish balconies and delicate fairy lights, wreaths on front doors handmade from pine trees and holly, buildings of red brick and dark wood. Abe's flat was set in a tall building overlooking the water, just a few streets away from Mr Cane's shoe shop. As they let themselves in through the foyer, the lights buzzed on and filled the front hall with yellow light.

"Top floor," Abe said, gesturing towards the stairwell. "Shall we?"

The stairs curved up the side of the building, dark and unyielding, and he led the way with his arms outstretched. The lights on each floor provided limited visibility, and Patrick clung to his coat in order to not lose his way.

"I'll just walk you to your door," he told Abe, though both of them knew they didn't want the night to end – not at the door, or ever in the future.

The very last apartment at the end of the corridor was locked, and as they slid the key into the lock and tumbled into the room, Patrick let out a gasp of surprise.

"I knew you were rich, but this is *crazy*!" He broke free of Abe and burst forwards, staring round at the room. "You actually *live* here?"

"I mean, just for the time being…"

"And – oh my *baubles*, look at the view!"

Patrick strode towards the double doors, fiddling with the catch before pulling them open. The moonlight from beyond shone in through the glass and enveloped them both, spilling across the floor as they stepped out onto the balcony.

"I wish my little sister could see this…" Patrick murmured, reaching to clutch the railings in awe. "She watches those Disney movies they like over on the continent.

We take her to the international cinema when we can afford to, and the opening credits are all ethereal and fancy. This is just like that."

Slowly, Abe walked towards him. Maybe it was the clock ticking past one behind him, or the comfort of his own space, but confidence had overwhelmed him; with shaking hands, he slipped an arm around Patrick's soft coat and held him there, by the waist, the softness of his body warm beneath his fingers.

"It's beautiful," Patrick whispered, turning his head slightly to look at Abe. "You're so lucky, getting to enjoy this every day."

"Yet I have no one to enjoy it with," Abe retorted, a little less jokily that he'd intended. He turned to Patrick guiltily. "Sorry. I guess… I guess I'm a bit bitter, living here alone."

"But you're not alone." Patrick's eyes were focused on him, like molten chocolate in the half-light. "You have me…"

Cautiously, an inch at a time, he lowered his head towards Abe.

And then he kissed him.

At first, Abe had no idea what was going on. It was like fireworks were going off in his head, six hundred per minute, exploding at a rate of knots against any logical thought. Soft, warm lips, pressing gently against his, tender against the corner of his mouth, the inside of his bottom lip, his teeth, the tip of his tongue.

He pulled away rapidly, pressing back against the railing and staring at Patrick with wide eyes.

"I'm sorry!" Patrick burst, cheeks flushed, breath quick. "I misjudged you, moved too fast, I… Abe, I'm so *sorry*."

But Abe just shook his head, heart still racing inside of him, the imprint of soft lips still warm against his own.

"It's okay," he managed. "I just…"

He glanced down at his hands, folded together in front of him.

He normally felt embarrassed about his previous lack of intimacy, but with Patrick, he felt so *safe*, unjudged. Like he could say anything, and still feel accepted.

"I've never kissed anyone before, see. And… you're a boy, one I kind of really like. It just surprised me."

"I should've known…" Patrick groaned, shuddering at his own stupidity. "You told me before that you hadn't been with anyone, and I should've taken it slower. I'll willingly leave now if you want me to, I promise."

Abe glanced up through his lashes. Patrick was staring down at him with a face of devastation, brown eyes soft and gentle, cheeks pink and rounded, fluffy hood framing his dark head of hair…

One foot still pressed against the railing, Abe took a step forward. Their heads were angled towards one another, skin bare against the cold air. Abe felt a warm arm curl round his back, strong and safe and *there*, as Patrick's body enveloped him and they collided in a mismatch of limbs and flesh and fabric, faces together and noses touching as they kissed, first slowly, then more urgently, against the balcony.

Then Patrick's lips were on his neck. They tingled like popping candy as they moved down, down his body, insistent, wanting more, craving. Abe knew being kissed was meant to feel good, but no one ever told him about the fireworks, the gooey feeling in your belly, the hands which never wanted to let go.

Said hands were in Patrick's hair, feeling around, touching his soft scalp, the back of his neck. Abe let out an involuntary moan as Patrick's lips found his collarbone, and the world erupted into a dazzling string of fairy lights around him.

I want you, he thought to himself, letting Patrick explore, nodding now, more certain than ever.

Because if this was what *being wanted back* felt like, Abe hoped it would never end.

Dear Patrick,

I'm writing this on a napkin as you use the bathroom. Maybe I'll give it to you at the end of the night, or maybe I'll keep it all for myself… as a reminder of how perfect this night has been, how perfect you are.

And no, this isn't those gorgeous mince pie cocktails talking. This is me, telling you that I like you. I really like you. You make me feel fizzy and special and seen. You make me feel exactly like… like champagne, or the special festive lemonade they sell down my old street.

I've never felt like this before, and I never want the thrill to end. Is that silly? Am I being silly?

Maybe. But I've spent my whole life being sensible, following the rules. Who says it's not time for me to break free now, to reject normal?

All my love,

Abe x

FIVE

The flat was warm as they moved inside, shutting the river behind glass doors and pulling the curtains closed. With two lamps casting a white-gold glow over the room, Abe pulled Patrick onto the sofa, where he perched on the edge with a wide, anxious smile.

"I know it's late, but you could stay the night, if you wanted?" He flushed red as soon as the words left his mouth, shaking his head in protest. "Not in that way! Just... on the sofa? If you don't want to walk home?"

Patrick smiled and sat down next to him, curving an arm around his waist and planting a kiss against the side of his face, so soft it was like the touch of a feather brushing his skin. His lips were light as they slipped down to his neck, lingering against his jaw, landing on his open collar.

"Are you warm?" he asked, glancing up at Abe shyly. With slow hands, Patrick reached to unbutton Abe's coat, pushing it off his shoulders and onto the sofa behind him. "That's better…"

He grazed Abe's shoulders with the tips of his fingers, running them down onto his bare arms, pale and translucent in the light of the lamps. Abe was still, simply staring at Patrick in wonder, heart racing as hands covered his body for the first time, intimate in a way he'd never experienced before, never dreamt of experiencing for real…

He was gentle as he tugged down the zip of Patrick's own coat, dragging it off to lie on the chair behind them. Patrick's belly sat against his hoody, which was soft and grey and cosy. As he was pulled towards it, Abe curled up into the fabric and nestled his chin on his chest.

"You smell of hot chocolate," he whispered. "With extra marshmallows and squirty cream…"

Patrick smiled, planting a kiss on the top of his head, then another on his forehead. "And you smell of mince pies, Abraham."

They continued to kiss as the night rolled on, feverish, still riled with passion, yet ever patient, careful. Surrounded by coats and cushions, they lay against the fabric of Abe's sofa, legs intertwined, the light of the lamp glowing on the table beside them. Their fingers were gentle, searching, fingers of careful exploration and first times, new and cautious. Patrick brushed the skin of Abe's stomach with his nail and Abe felt a shiver dart through him, a flush of cold ecstasy against the warmth of the room.

It wasn't like anything Abe had ever imagined, being close to Patrick like this. The movies they imported from Britain and America painted couples curled up around a Christmas tree, smiling and preened, with glossy white smiles and hair scooshed into perfect shape. They weren't gay elves, or lanky, pale twenty-year-old virgins, but beautiful people celebrating the most wonderful of Christmases. If they too were gay, they were shiny, pristine, perfect. Abe was none of those things.

But this, this was something else entirely. It wasn't perfect, shiny, covered in sparkles…

It was real.

The yellowing light; the rise of a hair against goosebumped skin; the gentle *tick-tock-tick* of the clock on the wall; a gentle moan, escaping from Patrick's lips. Two fingers, pressed into Abe's side, the skin of his lower back and hips. A warm, chocolatey scent, circling the room and slipping between their bodies like butter.

Patrick rubbed his nose gently against his; eyes closed, lashes splayed across coffee cheeks. The inhale of someone breathing in a candle, the tinkle of laughter, a naughty child breaking the silence of a school classroom.

"Tell me if you want to go to sleep…" he whispered, right into Abe's ear. But Abe shook his head, smiling, and prodded Patrick's stomach playfully.

As the sun came up, casting a vanilla glow over the river beyond, they watched the sky turn with eyes transfixed on the moving clouds. Patrick circled Abe's arm with his little finger, one stroke at a time, body arched around him like a cat, as the light of dawn shone through the rungs of the balcony's rail and spilt into the room.

Pinks, golds and blues struck the sky like lightning, a canvas of colours splattered by nature across her backdrop. A smattering of birds burst from a nearby building and tumbled across the sky in an eruption of black, stretching out against the clouds and flapping their wings as they raced towards the sun, further and further from the town down below, into the cold, early morning air.

"I've never seen the sunrise before," Abe murmured, into Patrick's chest. "I hate waking up early. I'm a total night person."

"We stayed up once," Patrick responded, "and watched the sunrise. Dora fell asleep, but David and I played games right until it was time to go to work. I didn't get much done that day. I kept falling asleep…"

It wasn't real, the sun rising in a perfect arc above them. It was just a fantasy, like the restaurant made of impenetrable gingerbread. Magic covered everything within the North Pole, creating an illusion of festive cheer, of normality, in a winter wonderland usually sunk into darkness. It was all a dream, from the happiness sprinkled over rooftops, to the decorations and lights filling their world.

But this – lying here, with Patrick, heart racing and skin buzzing with electricity – this was *more* than a dream. It was real, inside them, feelings flying through the air like sparks of yellow. It was more than just an illusion, the flicker of a memory. It was love, stark and raw, ripe for picking, ready to be grabbed with two hands and thrown into the real world.

"Abraham…" Patrick began, suddenly shy, tracing the lines of Abe's palm with a soft finger. "I know this might be too soon – we've only known each other one night, properly – but my grandparents have a cottage up in the mountains above the Jul Region, and they're staying with us over Christmas… so it'll be empty next weekend."

He was breathing heavily now, anxious for a reply, watching Abe.

"What I'm saying is… I'd like to spend the weekend with you, Abraham. Just the two of us. We've only just met, and yet… I've never felt like this before, not about anyone."

Abe was silent, blue eyes wide as he stared back.

"I…" Patrick faltered. "I think I'm falling in love with you, Abe."

They were silent as pink light flittered across their skin, pouring in through the sunlit window and speckling their joint hands. Patrick sucked in a breath and squeezed Abe's thumb, as if to comfort him, though his own heart was racing and he didn't dare make another noise.

It wasn't a statement Abe could take lightly. He'd never been in love before, never kissed a boy, never experienced anything close to what he felt right now. He'd never felt his heart flutter at the touch of two fingers, never held his breath as a nail gently rubbed his hips, setting off a thousand fireworks in his brain.

Was this love? How could he tell? He'd never felt it before, and had nothing to compare it to.

You couldn't fall in love with someone in under twenty-four hours, after just one date. He knew some people slept together on the first date, that one night stands were a thing, but *love*, that four-letter word so deeply entwined with family and forever and *permanency*... it wasn't possible, surely. That wasn't how it went in movies or in books. It wasn't how it had gone with his parents, with his grandparents, his peers...

All of the people who'd always made him feel inadequate for not having someone.

And yet Patrick's wording – *I'm falling in love with you* – just made so much *sense*.

He was burning up, turning to ash, a less-solid version of his former self. Melting into Patrick's arms, into his warmth, his soft belly and stony grey hoody. Collapsing into the comfort he felt when they talked, the way he could say anything, *be* anything, without judgement. It really was like falling; he couldn't stop himself from diving deeper and deeper.

"I think I'm falling in love with you too," he echoed. "It's not too soon."

Patrick was trying to hold back a smile, but it broke across his face in an electric beam. Abe couldn't help but grin back as he snuggled closer, tipping his head up to meet Patrick's.

"And I'd love to go to the cottage with you," he continued. "It sounds perfect."

More perfect than any tacky Christmas film he'd watched on his parents' imported TV, filled with fake white smiles and glittering Christmas trees.

It was perfect, because it was *real*.

Dearest Abraham,

Last night was incredible (morning – does it count as morning, seeing as we started at night?) and I've not stopped thinking about you ever since. I know we agreed it's not too soon, but the weight of the love I feel is... well, quite delicious, I suppose. All I want to do is take you back to the Gingerbread Restaurant and feed you mince pie cocktails until dawn, but for now, let's be satisfied with what we have.

The weekend away to the Jul Region. Have you ever been? My grandparents moved when they retired, and they're the loveliest people. They have the nicest little cottage in the mountains, but I don't want to tell you too much and spoil the surprise. It's the sweetest place. I have so many fond memories of days spent with my siblings in the snow, making snowmen and throwing snowballs and wandering off into a storm, just because.

I've included a kind of kit list at the back of this letter, because it's very important that you don't forget a thing. I know you're not daft, Abe, but seriously, this is going to be the best weekend ever. Depending on the snowfall, I want to show you all around the region, and do all of the best walks with you. You're a city boy, so I can't imagine you've seen much of the countryside. Am I being presumptive?

I also wanted to ask...

Are you telling your parents about this weekend? No pressure either way, because I totally don't want to out you. I just want to know that someone other than me knows where you are, in case they need to contact you or anything. You mentioned a best friend, Lottie. Have you told her?

Either way, I'm just so excited to spend the weekend with you! I've got so much planned, and I might have gotten my hands on the ingredients to make a big pot of that mince pie cocktail if you're interested in the likes of that... I know I certainly am.

I love you, and I can't wait to see you again. It already feels like it's been too long, and my chest aches at the thought of you.

Lots of love and sprinkles,
       Patrick xxx

SIX

"Where did you say you were going?" Mrs Cane asked, for the six hundredth time. They were stood in the kitchen of the family house, around the island, where she was making gingerbread men. As she rolled out the dough and looked at Abe in confusion, she said, "It was somewhere with Lottie, wasn't it?"

"That's right," Abe replied, reaching to steal a segment of dough. The sharpness of fresh ginger danced across his tongue. "We're going to a bed and breakfast place, just for two nights. It's up in the Jul Region, in the mountains."

Mrs Cane wrinkled her nose, unconvinced. "I don't see *why*," she said, sprinkling flour across her rolling pin. "Your father and I pay a fortune to rent that apartment for you, Abraham. Don't think we don't know what you're up to – it wouldn't be the first time a young man took his lady friend for a *rendezvous*, as it were."

"We're just friends, Mum." Abe rolled his eyes. "We fancied a change of scenery, that's all!"

"Friends, my backside!" His mother turned to raise the temperature on the Aga, frowning and shaking her head. "It's wrong, Abraham, it really is. Your father didn't take me to bed until the night of our wedding, which is the proper way to do things, in my book! It's an intimate thing, a special thing. You youngsters think you deserve pleasure at the shake of a stick." Abe cringed, as just as his mother added, "Make sure you use protection, anyhow. I'd be an irresponsible parent if I didn't tell you that…"

Hoisting his rucksack further onto his back, Abe turned around, so she couldn't see his flushed face. "I will, Mum. You don't have to tell me that. I'm an adult now."

An adult who was still very much a virgin and was absolutely *terrified* about what the weekend away might entail, yes.

But Mrs Cane didn't need to know that.

"Have a nice time, dear!" she called, as he opened the door and cold air flooded through the room. "Make sure you contact us when you're back, so that we know you're okay!"

"I will!" he shouted back, slamming the door behind him. "Bye, Mum!"

Outside, his old street was quiet. It was mid-afternoon and the residents were tucked into their front rooms, supping hot chocolate next to their Christmas trees. It was worlds away from the busy neighbourhood he now resided in, with its blocks of flats and cheerful river. Here, it felt like stepping back in time. Back to a childhood filled with middle-aged couples and their rich children, letter boxes and visits from Santa himself, metres from the school he'd grown up in.

He'd never cared that this was where he'd spent the first nineteen years of his life; it hadn't bothered him. But now, approaching Patrick at the street corner, he couldn't help but feel horribly… ashamed. There was nothing *wrong* with being privileged. But Abe hadn't recognised that that was what he was, until now.

"Hey!" Patrick burst, grinning and holding out his arms

for a hug. "It's so good to see you again!" Pulling back, he glanced around them. "It's so pretty around here, Abe! It's a little quiet though – doesn't it get boring?"

Abe shrugged. "It's just a bit... I don't know. Hardly anyone who lives here now is below the age of fifty, so you can imagine how that feels at Christmastime. They used to put on light displays, sell cookies in the front yards, that sort of thing... but now all the kids have moved out, this place is losing its sparkle. We're the first generation not to be moving back. The houses aren't worth as much anymore. My parents' house has gone down 50,000 coins in the last year."

Patrick pulled a face, linking his arm with Abe's. "That's the North Pole for you. All anyone wants is festive cheer."

They began to walk through the quiet residential streets to where the station was, right in the centre of the Noël Region. Leaving behind the neat houses with their perfect picket fences and glossy red doors, shops came into view, the nostalgic kind with hand-painted signs and dinky boxes of produce sat on turf-covered tables. Plump grapes hung from vines in the canopy above the greengrocer's, and across the street, Mr Cane's shoe shop sat among chocolate-box buildings.

"That's my dad's business," Abe explained, gesturing to the sign. "We fix up shoes, either imported from the continent or donated by people in the local area. They're given as Christmas presents for disadvantaged kids across the globe, so Santa pays a pretty good price for our services."

"Looks like you're all set," Patrick said, trying for a smile. "The perfect business, handed right to you."

Abe found himself blushing again, and hurried quickly to change the subject.

"What's the Natale Region like, then?" he asked. "I don't

think I've ever been."

"It's colourful!" Patrick responded, once again bubbly and giving a little jump for joy. The tension was cut and his arm squeezed tighter against Abe's. "It's full of stalls and food and festivity… we're big on street food and spices, and practically every house in the district has a deep fat fryer; we might have an Italian name, but the only vaguely Italian thing we eat on the daily is panettone. We cook a lot and host a lot of parties to make up for the work, though. There are factories at the end of most streets, and half of us work nights. I got lucky – day shifts, then a bit of work in the café on evenings, because my uncle knew the owner. It helps with the bills, see. Having four siblings isn't cheap."

"It sounds wonderful," Abe said, eyes wide. "Like a whole other world…"

"It's magical. We're like one big family. We all have each other's backs, you know? Everyone's so *accepting*."

"Even of…" Abe sucked in his breath. "Even of you being bisexual?"

"Of course!" Patrick smiled. "It's not as taboo as it is elsewhere. My boss on Tinsel Street couldn't believe it when David let slip, but no one at my old school cared. And if they did, they certainly wouldn't have *said* so."

"So why do people care so much about it over here?" Abe asked. "It's just not what elves do, that's what they say."

"I guess we're just more progressive there. Less traditional. There are bigger things to think about than *who* you love. There's more of a stigma around it here, I think. People are scared of change. I get that, though, you know? I just wish people on this side of town weren't so… I don't know the word." Patrick flushed, glancing sidewards at Abe. "Not you, of course. I mean, you're rich, but you're *certainly* not pretentious, if that's what you thought I was implying."

"It's okay. I am a *little* pretentious." Abe shoved Patrick playfully, then smirked and looked on ahead. "I mean, me and my parents *do* get invited to Santa's Christmas Ball each year. We're kind of in his inner circle, you may say."

Patrick just stared at him, eyes and mouth wide open. "You're... *friends* with Santa?"

"You could say so."

"And... you go to his *Christmas Ball*?"

"Every year."

Patrick shook his head in awe. "Golly, your parents are going to *hate* me."

Abe forced out a laugh.

Patrick, meet his parents? No chance. If he was ever going to introduce a boy to them, one from the Natale Region wouldn't even be considered.

But he didn't want to think about that, now.

The train station sat on a junction. It was an imposing building, made of the same red brick as Abe's apartment block, laced with a trim of festive green carvery. A tree sat outside, too tall to have been grown without magic, decorated with baubles and candles and gold and red tinsel. Elves ran about outside, smiling and waving, clutching briefcases full of toy designs and recipe ideas as they hurried about their business.

There was a coffee shop inside; Patrick treated them both to gingerbread lattes and chocolate chip cookies wrapped in brown paper, still gooey from the oven. They ate them on a bench at the edge of the platform, beneath the latticed ceiling, watching the world go by as they gorged on soft dough. Suitcases, takeout coffees and bags of snacks were piled onto the huge steam trains rolling in and out of the station, breasts gleaming beneath the station's lamps and smoke swirling into the wide ceiling space to stain the glass grey.

"We hardly ever use the train," Patrick whispered, right in Abe's ear. "It's way too expensive. But this is my Christmas present to myself."

"I would've paid –" Abe began, but Patrick put a hand up to stop him.

"As I said, this is *my* present. And it's my money, and I want to spend it on today, okay?"

The chalkboards on the station's walls kept writing and rewriting themselves, announcing new train times. Abe checked his watch against the time before him, and nudged Patrick with an elbow.

"It's our train next," he said. "Get ready!"

When their train pulled into the station, a magnificent beast of glossy red and forest green, they were the first up the steps. The seats inside were brown and warm, and tinsel hung between each aisle in a festive zigzag. Patrick sat opposite with a table between them, and nudged Abe's foot gently.

"It's beautiful, isn't it?" he asked, smiling. "All this Christmas cheer. I'll never tire of it."

Abe smiled, but he couldn't meet Patrick's eyes. Truth be told, this was the first year he'd properly enjoyed the spectacle of it all. After he came out all those years ago, this time of year had lost its sparkle. It was the busiest time of the year, a time when his parents were stressed and businesses all over the North Pole burst with their efforts to get ready for Santa's journey.

They took Christmas *way* too seriously, especially in Noël. And amidst all of the worry, the wonder got lost, slightly.

The train rolled out of the station, making its way steadily through the North Pole. The sun shone down in all its magical glory, from somewhere beyond their realm, a place which didn't exist outside of a dream. The Noël Region twisted into the greying factories of the Natale Region, where the smog was barely penetrated by the Christmas spirit. Despite the dark streets, Abe could see what Patrick had meant; each house was decorated, with stalls and lights and smiling snowmen parked along the pavements, elves smiling out of windows at the children playing outside.

The Natale Region soon broke into broad daylight, where cascading hills glistened with white snow and a cloudless blue sky screamed with joy. The Jul Region: a mountainous expanse of land, where greenhouses grew all of their Christmassy essentials… with the help of Santa's magic, of course.

And beyond that – further than any elf had ever ventured, or ever *could* venture – the magic cut off, giving way to a dark, desolate Arctic, devoid of the Christmas spirit, empty of life. They couldn't leave, and no one could see in, keeping the secret of the North Pole. Should any human attempt to find them, they'd find the same, empty stretches of land seen from above. The only gesture to the existence of Santa and his elves was a pinprick of light, like a star; their artificial sun, hung high up in the sky, casting light upon the North Pole all year round, leaving them in darkness as night fell.

Abe took a deep breath, resting his head against the window as he gazed out at the landscape.

He'd never felt so happy in all his life.

Dear Patrick,

I'm so excited to go on this trip with you. Your grandparents' cottage sounds so cute. Are you close to them? And I assume they're fine with you using their house to host… well, me?

I've really enjoyed getting to know you, you know. This all feels like a dream.

And I love you, too. It still feels strange to write that, like it's not really real. Because how can it be? You're far too good for me. I never in a million years dreamt that a boy like you would ever want someone like me.

You're perfect, and I love you.

I love you. I'm going to keep writing that, you know, and it'll probably never feel exhausted.

All my love,

        Abe x

SEVEN

The train pulled into the station late that afternoon, collapsing with a lonely *hiss* beside the platform. The sky was inky blue above them as they stepped out into the cold air, coats wrapped around them against the chill, ice creeping through the soles of Abe's felted mules.

"We'll have to walk up to the cottage," Patrick said, pulling a face. "I don't have the money for a cab, but it's not that far…"

"Then it's my treat," Abe cut in.

They hailed one right outside the station, a hansom cab pulled by a white horse, tossing his mane and snorting as he made his way through the snow towards them. The driver doffed his cap and gestured for them to climb on up, beaming. Abe led the way. He reached up awkwardly to grab the railings, hoisting himself into the seat.

"Smooth." Patrick smirked, hopping in beside him. "Real smooth."

The seats were soft and black, covered by a canopy of brown, as they set off into the gathering evening. Abe felt himself snuggle closer into Patrick. The Jul Region was a rural area, the main body made up of villages and farms set along the mountainside; cottages full of retirees sat in culs-desac or at the edge of forests. Each surface was covered in a thick slab of snow, and tendrils fell from the sky under a cool fog. Thatched roofs, red letterboxes and white picket fences decorated the scene, trapped under an ever-darkening sky studded with stars. Streetlamps cast a yellow glow onto the pavements below, indistinguishable against the snow-covered road, and tracks and horseshoe prints led down the winding streets, telling the story of travellers from a time before.

Abe breathed in the cool air, letting it fill his mouth, his lungs, his heart.

Patrick's grandparents lived in a cottage outside of the village, up a track which led around the mountain. The driver and horse could barely see the road ahead for swirling snow and craggy rocks. Patrick and Abe clung to each other, the storm battering the cab and crushing their bodies together as fierce winds blew in every direction. Bumps in their path were inevitable, yet the strong white horse continued, whinnying and kicking his feet in cold anguish.

If they could see further than a few metres through the thick smog, they'd have noticed a severe drop to their left, where the road crumbled away and the mountainside sloped into a steep smile. But they couldn't see a thing. In fact, they were so wrapped up in trying to stay close, huddling in their coats in the back of the hansom cab, that they were hardly aware of the scenery around them.

"Where did you say you wanted dropping?" the driver shouted, turning his head to read their lips. His cheeks were purple with cold, burst blood vessels standing out like the lines of a map across his nose and forehead.

"Mistletoe Cottage!" Patrick called back. He twisted his neck back to meet Abe's gaze, smirking. "Very apt."

The cab pulled to a stop at the highest point, where the

road was stopped by two large wooden slabs.

"It's been blocked off – they must've had an avalanche ahead!" The driver was frowning, as he turned around to speak to them properly. "If you really want to get there tonight, you'll have to walk, boys! There should be way round the snow by foot, if you're willing to risk it. There's a lamp somewhere back there, should light up if you tap it hard enough…"

Patrick ducked his head to feel around his feet on the cab's floor. Finding a gas lamp, he picked it up and pulled it onto his lap, where Abe gave it a significant whack and they both watched as a flame flickered from within.

"Excellent!" The driver beamed. "And seeing as it's Christmas and I haven't delivered you straight there, the ride is on me. If you need picking up at the end of the weekend, I'll be driving this way on Sunday at one. I'm taking old Mrs Higgins to get her shopping!"

"That's great!" Patrick responded, leaning forward to shake his hand. "You're a good elf!"

The driver shook his head, but he was smiling widely and leapt out to help them with their bags, slapping Abe on the back as he went.

"You boys have fun! Don't be doing anything I wouldn't do…"

They watched, huddled together against the snowfall, as the hansom cab slid away into the night. It was pitch black now, the only light coming from their dismal little lamp, which lit up the falling snow for a short length before flittering into nothing.

"How are we supposed to get there in this weather?" Abe asked, teeth chattering. "We can't see anything!"

"It's okay…" Patrick replied. "I remember where we are, I

think. There's this point on the road that always suffers avalanches from the forest above, and Granddad keeps those boards right by it, just in case. The cottage isn't too far away!"

"But I'm wearing *felted mules*!" Abe protested. "I can barely feel my feet as it is!"

"We'll be there soon," Patrick reassured him, slipping an arm around his waist and taking a tentative step forward into the snow. "Besides… I can warm you up."

Abe's stomach flipped at that, a cosy feeling settling in his core.

They were slow and cautious as they advanced towards the cottage, slipping over the snow and clambering up the avalanche to meet the road again, dodging rocks and cowering against the storm with hoods held firmly over their heads and scarves wrapped tight. Their surroundings swam in a mass of snow-flecked black, broken only by the weak light of the lamp.

"Only a bit longer, Abe. We're almost there…"

But Abe was too cold to comprehend Patrick's words.

When a thatched roof and white wall came into view before them, the shadow of a building, Patrick let out a whoop of joy and squeezed Abe tight against him. Shivering violently and with feet like blocks of ice, they forced the last few steps up the path, until the light from the lamp lit up a flaking red door. Patrick's numb fingers fumbled with the lock until the door creaked open, and they tumbled inside.

"Take your shoes off," Patrick instructed, slamming the door behind them. With the snow trapped outside, the roaring storm locked away, it was like they'd entered a whole other world, and Abe sunk to the floor in relief.

The room was wide and open plan, the walls made of exposed brick, beams connecting the sloping ceiling. A light fluttered from the middle of the room, high up in a candleholder, and at one end, a fire soon crackled behind a guard. Abe pulled off his sopping mules and kicked them across the wooden floor, then proceeded to pull off his snow-dusted coat and scarf, dropping them into a pile beside him.

"Go and sit by the fire. I'll take care of your bags."

Although Abe wanted to help, he was simply too cold; he watched as Patrick carried the rucksack and suitcase to the bottom of the stairs, before shuffling to the hearth on his bottom.

The fireplace was huge, towering above him in a mismatch of coloured tiles. Before it lay an orange, blue and purple rug, made from tiny pieces of material threaded through a hessian sack, something Patrick's grandmother had probably handmade long ago. He collapsed against it with his hands beneath his head and watched the flames flicker before him as warmth seeped through his body.

"Comfy?" a voice murmured, from just behind him. Two hands curved round his waist, warm and soft, like cookie dough, malleable against him. Arching his back, he found Patrick's body and sunk into him instinctively, like warm milk spilling over them both, connecting them beneath an invisible membrane.

As Patrick leaned over him, one leg between his, Abe opened his eyes. Patrick's hair fell over his forehead in a soft, dark ball of fluff, eyes wide and smiling, like chocolate truffles, lips plump and perfect, cheeks blemish-free and the colour of a latte made just right.

How could anyone be so completely and utterly *flawless*?

He tipped his head up to meet Patrick's, feeling sunshine roll through him as their lips touched, gently, noses resting side by side. He went back again, more urgently this time, teeth latched onto his bottom lip and nibbling feverously. The soft warmth of Patrick's mouth against his; a tongue, twisting further into his own, running along his gums and stroking the insides of his cheeks with desperate patience.

A finger stroked the base of his stomach, so close to the waistband of his trousers, and a shiver ran through him.

"You're still all wet from the storm," Patrick whispered. "You can't get warm wearing these clothes…"

With trembling fingers, he took hold of Abe's t-shirt by the hem and tugged it until it was off and over his head. Eyes transfixed on the white of his stomach, the stretched canvas of skin over his ribs, his shoulders, his flat stomach and twin nipples, Patrick couldn't prevent his hands from reaching out…

Abe inhaled deeply as fingers met his flesh, roaming across his bare stomach, his chest, his shoulders.

"Oh, Patrick…"

He let out a gasp, just audible, escaping through his parted lips as Patrick's hands moved across his abdomen and teased the line of his belt, the skin just above. Shaking, he reached forward to drag the arms of Patrick's hoody over his hands and up into the air, discarding it on the rug beside them. And then – *oh*.

Bare flesh, light brown sugar; lightning bolts along his waist, chocolatey stretch marks he wanted to press his lips against; soft folds of stomach and chest; wiry hairs, pointing out from beneath the hollows of his armpits. Patrick's cheeks were flushed pink as he let Abe take him in, fighting the urge to cover himself with his hands.

"You look…" But Abe couldn't get his words out.

"Hideous?" Patrick suggested. "Like a great fat lump? Disgusting? Jelly –"

"Stop!" Abe placed a finger on Patrick's lips, feeling them against his hand like overripe bananas. "You're... you're breathtaking."

Behind them, the fire continued to crackle, and the beams above creaked with pressure from the storm outside. Patrick's expression was one of abject surprise as Abe leaned closer, a smile dancing across his face, to whisper in his ear.

"And... I know I said I was falling in love with you, but..." He glanced away in mock distress. "I was wrong."

Patrick frowned, eyebrows creasing as he cocked his head to one side.

"I'm not falling anymore," Abe whispered, leaning forwards to close the gap. "You've caught me, Patrick. You've blooming well caught me."

Dearest Abe,

God, if I were a writer I'd be able to put into words how I feel about you, but I'm not, so I'm trying my hardest. No words do you justice, Abraham Cane.

One day, I'll have a whole bundle of letters to give to you, all about my love for you, how incredible I think you are.

Am I naïve in thinking we'll be together forever, that when we're eighty-five, I can lean over in our little mountain cottage and pass you the letters, tell you how I loved you all along, from the very moment I saw you?

I remember watching this play once – a Shakespeare, I think, it was with school – and scorning first love. It seemed so silly, and so shallow. But I understand it all now.

It's more than attraction. It's knowing, feeling, sensing. You know when you meet the one. I knew. I hope you knew, too. I think you did. I'm pretty certain.

Lots of love and sprinkles,
        Patrick xxx

EIGHT

They woke up the next day in front of the fire, light pouring in through the cottage's latticed windows. Patrick's arms were wrapped around Abe's waist and stomach, Abe's hands all in his hair, resting at the back of his neck. The baubles of light splattered across the floorboard were interrupted by a smattering of snow, still falling against the chilly mountainside.

"Morning," Patrick mumbled, into Abe's nose. "Yuck, I don't want to speak to you. I get such bad morning breath…"

Opening his eyes groggily, Abe's face was just a few centimetres from Patrick's. He could see every detail of his cheeks, plump lips, dark eyelashes, in high definition before his eyes.

"I don't care," he whispered, leaning forward to kiss him. "Mine's even worse…"

They found food in the larder for breakfast, which they ate at the big table to the side of the room. Crusty bread with chicken liver pâté; cranberry juice in big teal mugs; cornflakes, without the milk. It was chilly in the kitchen, the floorboards like ice beneath their feet, so they wrapped up warm in big blankets and hats as they sat on the bench and gazed out of the window at the snowy hillside below.

How could it possible get better?

A little later, Patrick pulled Abe to his feet, the grin on his face gentle, teasing. Pulling on their coats and some of the wellies found in the cupboard beside the larder, Patrick and Abe bounded out into the sunshine as eleven ticked by. The ground was untouched, aside from the pawprints of an Arctic fox, decorated from bush to bush in a smattering of imprints. The snow sparkled in the sunlight, glinting like the glitter of a bauble, the perfect fabric for a wedding dress or fir trim.

Dropping to the ground, Patrick lay back on the snow with the biggest smile on his face, gazing up at Abe in adoration.

"Me and my siblings always do this at Christmastime!" he explained, pushing his arms out and moving them up and down, forming perfect wings on the ground around him. "Come on, join me!"

Abe fell to his knees, feeling the cold seep through the legs of his chinos. Flopping onto his back beside Patrick, he raised his arms above his head, kicked out his feet and began to dance against the snow, drawing the perfect fairy ballgown beneath him.

"My parents never used to let me play like this!" he shouted over his shoulder. "They were worried about me ruining my clothes, or getting hypothermia – something like that, anyway."

Standing up and linking hands, they gazed at their imprints beneath them, one big and one small, laid together in perfect unity.

"Snow fairies," Patrick whispered. "Perfect."

The day fell in front of them in a timeline of freedom and adventure. They scoured the mountainside in their wellies and thick clothing until their fingers were numb and they couldn't feel their feet. Snow fell throughout, a light dusting of icing sugar on the ground around them, falling through a sieve in soft, miniscule balls. The boys tipped their heads up to the sun and caught flakes in their mouths, eyelashes, hair, feeling the delicate pinpricks dance along frozen skin.

They ate fresh berries come dinnertime, cold and yet ripe from the bushes around the cottage; magical pockets of wonder, exploding inside of their mouths. In a world of ice and death and bare, lonesome trees, the fruit-bearing bushes glinted as they held their secret close.

The ground around the cottage was soon trampled and rugged as Patrick and Abe rushed across the snow, throwing snowballs and shrieking with laughter, rolling smaller clumps to form the body of an elaborate snowman. Mr Icing was a fine specimen, tall and made of tightly packed flakes, a smattering of stones for buttons and two thick arms carved around his belly.

"No doubt he'll get all the snowladies chasing after him," Abe said, pressing the final pebble into place on his smiley mouth.

Patrick rolled his eyes, poking his arm. "Or snow*men*."

He disappeared inside the cottage a little later, producing a baguette and a huge baked camembert atop a wooden board, so unnecessarily extravagant that Abe couldn't help but burst out with laughter at the sight of him crossing the snow. The board was placed in the centre of the picnic table they'd commandeered, the cheese dipped into with eager hands and generous slices of bread. Abe found red onion chutney at its centre, gooey and oozing. Soft, white dough against melted, garlic-y camembert, dissolving against their tongues as they lapped up the meal in silence.

Several more snow fairies were formed as the day dragged on, creating a school of tiny creatures imprinted in the snow. Mr Icing gained a Mrs Icing, a voluptuous women Patrick had far too much fun sculpting the breasts of. Two large clumps of snow later, she'd gained nipples and the most magnificent bust.

"If you're so attracted to those snow boobs, maybe I should give Mr Icing some more detail," Abe suggested, scowling.

"Ooh, yes please!" Patrick burst, beaming with eyes wide. "I'll help!"

At that, Abe faux-huffed and pretended to stomp away from him.

They stayed outside until the sun melted away against the North Pole's shiny edge; golden red, fiery orange, buttery yellow. Sat against the cottage's walls with their bottoms wet and cold and eyes aglow, they watched the sky fade, first from blue to vermillion, then from vermillion to thick, dark black, like ink. An Arctic fox, formed perfectly from delicate white fur and beady eyes, tiptoed across the ground before them, reprinting his route. Above them, birds disappeared into their trees for the night in a rippling of wings and caws.

They clutched hands tight beneath their sleeves, and Abe nestled gently into Patrick, nose pressed against his cold neck.

"I love you," he murmured, just quiet enough that Patrick could make out his words. There was no more that needed to be said – that was the line, the result of their day in the snow, all either of them ever needed to be sure of.

When it was too cold to remain and the sun had well and truly set, the boys stood on shaky feet and made their way inside the cottage. Like the previous night, it was warm and dry and light, the fire crackling in its pompous hearth behind a raggedy rug. Pulling off their wet clothes, they rummaged in their suitcases for dry ones, Abe trying his hardest not to look in Patrick's direction…

But he couldn't help it. The soft skin of Patrick's stomach folded over itself in all its coffee-coloured glory, rippling over a pair of light blue boxers. They were the perfect amount of tight, just showing the slim outline of his…

Abe turned away, flushing, and tugged on his own fleecy bottoms in haste.

Crashing beside the fire for one more night, Patrick pulled Abe closer, wrapping an arm tight around his shoulders and kissing the side of his neck. All limbs and lips and wild, firelit eyes, they curled up against Patrick's grandma's rug, hearts racing and tongues hurried, desperate.

"I don't think we should sleep in front of the fire again," Patrick whispered, against Abe's nose. "It gave me a bad back. My grandparents' room is just upstairs…"

Confidence soaring inside his anxious heart, Abe smiled, rising onto his feet. He held out a hand to Patrick in order to help him up, and said, "Shall we?"

The stairs of the cottage were rickety and curved around the side of the building, and each step creaked as they made their way upwards. There wasn't much of a hallway, simply a stretch of landing leading to various rooms, which Patrick explained to be the spare bedrooms and bathroom, which his own family would inhabit upon coming to stay.

"My mum's bedroom only has a small bed," he explained. "My younger siblings always bunk in with her in their cots and on the spare mattress, so it's a bit naff, really."

At the end of the corridor was the tallest door, made of solid pine and shut tight. Pushing down on the handle, Patrick gently opened the door and stepped into the room with Abe in tow.

"And this," he said, raising a seductive eyebrow with a grin, "is the master bedroom."

It was a heavy room, full of dark wood panelling and bold patterns. Huge curtains fell from the window in plum, gold and apricot, forming a pattern of swirling leaves and flowers embroidered onto a shimmering green backdrop. The rugs covering the exposed wooden planks were fluffy and deep purple, and tickled the undersides of their feet as they crossed the floor.

In the very centre of the room was a four-poster bed, carved out of the same dark wood and with curtains that accented those by the windows, edged in gold brocade. The covers were a dark peach colour, the pillows the same, two ochre cushions sat in the very centre. A real fur blanket lay across the end of the bed; it looked like the fur of a wolf, dark grey and brown, with streaks of white.

Perching on the edge of the bed, Patrick gazed up at Abe with obliging brown eyes. The atmosphere had shifted completely. They were no longer rushing about in the snow, or curled up by the crackling fire.

They were on a bed in a cold room, wearing *pyjamas*, and the air between them was electric.

As a sudden burst of desire rippled through him, Abe threw himself at Patrick. Legs curling around his waist and hands all in his hair, he sat against his partner on the edge of the bed, in his lap, his arms, his belly.

He kissed him in a way they never had before, a way that sent sparks surging across his chest and abdomen, hot flakes of snow dancing over his thighs and neck and arms, flying through his mind like electricity.

They kissed and kissed as Patrick fell backwards and the

bed swallowed them whole. Trapped together, body heat radiating through their furry tent, Abe had never felt so alive; every inch of his body was pulsating with love and ecstasy.

And then Patrick's hands were on his stomach again, soft and careful and warm, rubbing his belly button, hips, right down to the waistband of his fleecy bottoms. With tender care, he tugged on them, until they were off and out of the bed altogether.

Now, bare legs against bare legs, Abe's heart wouldn't stop. It was almost like it had wings and would at any moment take flight, rising right out of his throat and across the mountains away from him.

Two fingers, pressing against his boxers, pulling gently on the seam…

A hand, grasped around them, dragging them down, down, over his knees, his ankles…

It was freezing in the cottage's master bedroom, but Abe had never felt warmer. Every inch of him was quivering as he reached towards Patrick, heart running faster and faster, right up his throat…

They were both naked, the two of them, lost in their most vulnerable state. Abe had always pictured this moment with nerves, but there was nothing to be nervous about as he felt Patrick's fingers on his flesh, squeezing down, eyes roaming his body, searching.

They repositioned themselves, minds and bodies in sync. Abe could swear the sound of his heart beating was so loud you could've heard it from outside the door.

Was this real?

Was any of it?

"Abraham Cane…" were the last words to leave Patrick's lips, before Abe's mind was overtaken by a swarm of bright blue butterflies.

Flying, soaring…

Flapping their wings, electric in the light of a bright blue sky.

Dear Patrick,

(I will never send this letter, because I think it's a little too vulnerable, even for me.)

Whenever I thought about losing my virginity before, it was always a kind of hazy concept. I don't think I ever really knew what it would look like, except for the vision indoctrinated in me by cheesy American films (you know which one I mean, Mr and Mrs Terminal Elfness – I see you) or books about first love and sex. It was very clinical and cold, a procedure, because I knew I didn't like girls but I didn't know I liked boys, and the confusion made me stop thinking about sex at all.

I never thought I'd be twenty years of age when I lost my virginity, either. That's another thing the media tells us. That we'll be teenagers when we take a leap of faith and have The Sex, the big ol' sexy sex, the intercourse that's meant to make us hurt and cry and bleed.

But the thought of insecure little Abe, sixteen and shivering, being so vulnerable with someone…

It makes me want to cry.

While virginity is a social construct in and of itself, there's something horribly bare and intimate about any act of sex, no matter what it is. Whether it's the kind we were taught at school, age eleven, with flushed cheeks and bleary eyes, or the kind we learnt through magazine problem pages at thirteen, fourteen, realising for the first time that you might not be like all the other boys… it is a big deal. It's scary, and it's intense. And even if it doesn't hurt, it feels like something is breaking inside of you when it's all done.

But with Patrick, it felt right. That's what I can say, confidently, in the moments after, sat here in the living room, thinking things over, ready to go back to bed and cuddle up with him under the sheets. It felt right, and it felt like it was worth the wait. Like he was worth the wait.

Because at the end of the day… love was worth the wait.

All my love,

        Abe x

NINE

Awaking in Patrick's arms beneath the heavy duvet, Abe stretched his arms above his head, until they poked out against the cold air. It was Sunday, their last day in the cottage, and yet his whole body was beaming.

"I had sex last night," he said to the air. It didn't matter that no one was listening, or that Patrick was still snoring against him. He needed to get it out of his system.

Crawling out of bed seemed like the least awkward option at this point, seeing as he was stark naked and lying right next to someone he assumed was now his *boyfriend*. In the heat of the moment, bare flesh hadn't seemed like such a big deal; Patrick's body against his was a luxury he never thought he'd afford, like liquid gold between them under the sheets. It still looked that way now, in the cold light of day, every detail clear, crystal clear.

He dislodged his body from its position near Patrick, pushing his arm away. Trying to be quiet and not shift the covers too much, he lifted a leg over the edge of the bed, when a snort came from behind him and Patrick's messy head popped up from where it was laid against the pillow.

"Morning," he grumbled, shaking his head and yawning. "We don't have to get up yet, do we?"

"I…" Abe faltered. He didn't want to lie to Patrick, and yet he already felt so uncomfortable, perched there with no clothes on as light flittered through the latticed windows. "I was just going to get some food. Do you want anything?"

"There's some bacon in the larder. Use up the rest of that baguette, I don't think it'll keep…"

Abe hovered for a moment, before turning to face him. Patrick's hair was stuck up in all directions, brown eyes tired, lids sagging around them and edged with sleep. He looked adorable, bare chest and shoulders just visible, gazing out at him hopefully.

"I'll go make breakfast." Abe flushed, gesturing towards the door, Patrick's bottom lip jutted out as he said this, cocking his head to one side in order to seem upset.

"You're going right away?" he asked. "Aw, come on Abe. We don't leave until later! Get back in bed…"

Suggestively, Patrick tugged the duvet down, exposing more of his chest and stomach, just below.

Abe blushed even darker red.

"Just ten more minutes," Patrick murmured. "Then I'll come and help make breakfast."

Despite the nerves pulsing through him, Abe couldn't resist tunnelling back under the covers and into Patrick. Feeling their skin connect in an instantaneous chemical reaction, he reached to kiss his partner, his love, taking his head in his hands and kissing, kissing, right down the side of his face and body until he met the soft flesh of his lower abdomen…

Patrick let out a moan from somewhere above him, a sound of what Abe could only identify as pleasure, relief. Lying back, he couldn't stop the smile from spreading across his face, for it was *he* who'd made Patrick feel like that, brought such joy to him, such happiness. If he could spend the rest of his life doing the same, he'd be content. It was all he needed.

They made their way down to make breakfast a while later, still fuzzy and warm, despite the cold of the cottage. The main space downstairs was warmer, as the fire crackled on in all its magical glory, logs still intact below the orange flames.

Patrick was now in those light blue boxer shorts, stomach flopping lazily over the waistband, and Abe had wrapped up tight in his dressing gown. They moved around the kitchen in amicable silence, the window letting in soft sunlight. Abe fried the bacon while Patrick toasted the baguette, and they combined the two over the big wooden table. They only had a few hours left now, before the driver would pick them up and they'd be carried back towards the village in the hansom cab.

Overnight, Mr Icing and his voluptuous wife seemed to have sagged slightly, and were now sloping dramatically sidewards.

"She seems to have... aged." Patrick smirked, while Abe rolled his eyes and began to collect up the dishes, filling the sink with hot, soapy water. "All my handiwork, ruined..."

Their bags were packed and waiting by the door, and Abe felt a jolt of sadness run through him as he tugged his backpack up and onto his shoulders. If only they could stay here forever, away from the North Pole's prying eyes. But for now, until he arrived back home in the familiar Noël Region, he wanted to forget about everything else and just enjoy *Patrick*, because who knew how long it'd be until they could have this time together again.

The cab driver met them down by the avalanche, and doffed his cap cheerfully in their direction.

"Good weekend, boys?" he called. "You're looking very

rosy-cheeked!"

They set off down the mountainside at a steady pace, a gentle breeze blowing through the cab's front, yet not at all like it had done during their arrival. It looked so much more beautiful in the daylight, the whole of the Jul Region laid out before them in a mismatch of thatched cottages, frozen rivers and steady pines, smiling up like the perfect model village, steam train huffing and puffing throughout. The sky was blue and unbroken, and birds chirped in the branches above.

They picked up Mrs Higgins outside of her farm, to take her to the shops. Patrick helped her up with a gentlemanly hand and she beamed at him gratefully, settling between them like a collapsing plum pudding, rippling over the seat with her large posterior and flowing skirts.

"You must be Betty and Boris's grandson," she said, poking a finger at Patrick. "I'm a good friend of Betty's, see. She told me all about you. This young man must be your special friend, then? My, how I'd have loved a little hideaway for me to take my fancy men, back in the day…"

"It's a very romantic part of the world," Patrick replied, smirking at Abe. "Especially at Christmas!"

"Ooh, I don't doubt it, love, I don't doubt it. If only Mr Higgins was still alive, I'd have someone to enjoy it with…" Mrs Higgins pressed her chin down against her chest sadly, causing it to double in size. "But I had my fun, back in the day. Your granddad, he was the one they all wanted, Patrick. Ask him if he remembers that day in the barn, on his Christmas holiday in nineteen-sixty… what year was it? I kept him warm then, no doubt I did…"

Patrick pulled a horrified face at Abe, who was trying too hard not to laugh to be of much help.

The village rolled into view in the nick of time, and they

both helped Mrs Higgins out when they reached the shops, waving her on her way. She moved away from them like a swaying pair of curtains, and, as she disappeared through the sliding doors, they smiled at each other and hopped back up into the cab.

"To the station!" the driver shouted, grinning at them both. "It'll be my pleasure!"

Their train left in half an hour, but being a small station, there weren't the refreshment outlets or coffee houses of the town centre. The cab driver treated them to hot bagels from a stall instead, and they ate them together, sat on the wall outside. Steaming, buttery dough melted on their tongues and warmed them from the inside, setting fire to the cold day.

"Thank you so much for everything!" Patrick called. "If only we could repay you somehow…"

"Don't worry about it!" the driver responded. Abe was watching, silent, unsure of how to say thank you himself. "Truth be told, I have a son who recently came out. My wife was so unsure at first, but… I love my son. I could never hate him for something he can't control, like who he loves. And I can tell you two must've needed somewhere safe to go, and I hope my own son will always feel safe to tell me when he needs somewhere to go, you know?"

Patrick and Abe were speechless for a second, before Patrick wordlessly shook his hand.

"Thank you," he said, nodding his head. "If only all fathers were like you, Sir."

They caught the train ten minutes later, and waved out the window at the cab driver as they pulled away from him. This was it. They'd reached the end of their trip, and in a few hours, they'd be leaving each other for the first time in three days.

Abe was still trying not to think about that part.

The Jul Region glittered in the afternoon sun as greenhouses danced past in all their shining glory, cottages and tiny picket fences twisting into the dark shape of the Natale Region, streets dark and cold beneath the smog, children building snowmen from coal-stained snow. Patrick turned his head away from the window as they passed it, frowning, but Abe couldn't drag his eyes from the smut-covered houses with their brashly painted front doors.

"Almost home," he said, turning to Patrick. "It feels rubbish to be back, doesn't it?"

"I'll see you soon!" Patrick promised, and they nudged feet beneath the table in order to cement it. "I can't *not* see you, Abe. It's like… an addiction. I'll come to your apartment as often as I can."

As the train pulled to a stop in the Noël station, they picked up their bags and began to disembark. The station was full of elves who rushed into arms, towards signs, hugging and kissing and crying as the sound echoed against the glass roof. Abe lugged Patrick's suitcase from the storage space at the bottom of the train – when from behind them came a desperate, strangled cry.

"*Abraham Cane!*"

Gulping and twisting around, Abe came face to face with his mother.

She was stood before him with her handbag hoisted atop her shoulder, staring at him with a wide open mouth and huge, distraught eyes. Glancing from Abe to Patrick, then back to Abe again, she shook her head desperately, as if to erase what she was seeing.

"I can explain, Mum –" Abe begin, but she cut him off with another bedraggled yelp.

"Gerald! Gerald, oh Gerald, please help me!"

Mr Cane jogged over in an instant, Lottie hot on his heels. She met Abe's eyes with a guilty smile, but he couldn't return it, for every part of his body was burbling with what felt like *anger*.

"He was with this boy the whole time!" his mother was exclaiming, pointing at Patrick with a horrified finger. "Not only did he lie to us, Gerald, but he was with this – this *boy* – the entire weekend!"

"Is this true, son?" Mr Cane asked, whilst Abe sweltered under his gaze. "Were you really with this... *elf*?"

Abe opened his mouth to speak, but the words seemed lodged in his throat.

"When you didn't send a fast-tracked letter to tell us you were okay, we *had* to go and see Lottie," Mrs Cane explained. "The poor dear can't lie to save her life, we all know that. Well, it was clear you weren't with her in the Jul Region, and when she told us you were there with someone else, we were immediately suspicious." She shook her head again, tears filling her eyes. "How *dare* you, Abraham? After everything we've given you, to just throw it back in our faces like that. Do you have no respect?"

"I'm sorry," he started, but his parents had already turned their attention to Patrick.

"And you," Mrs Cane continued, jabbing her long nail right at Patrick's eye, "don't your parents control you *at all*? Or are they so disgusted by your... your *preferences* that they've disowned you altogether?" She was shaking now, hand quivering as she tried to hold it steady. "And you, Abe... you've let us down again."

"Excuse me, but I hardly think –"

But Mrs Cane wouldn't let Patrick speak. "Come on,

Gerald. Tell Abraham what we talked about."

Abe's father squirmed uncomfortably, then glanced at him with shifty eyes which said it all.

"The thing is…" he began. "We need someone to continue the business, Abe. So, if you're… if you're *homosexual*, and you don't carry on the Cane line, then we can't give you the shop."

And right there in the station, a week into December, stood next to the boy he'd just fallen in love with, Abe's world completely and utterly collapsed.

Dear Abe,

I'm so sorry.

I'm sorry that your parents don't understand you. I'm sure they're good people deep down, but I'm sorry they don't want to listen to you, or even try to learn.

I'm sorry that I didn't fight back. I wasn't sure if it was what you wanted.

I'm sorry I couldn't stop them from hurting you.

I'm sorry I didn't grab your arm and try to pull you back, pull you into me. I'm sorry I wasn't enough in that moment. You can hate me for it, I'll understand.

I'm sorry I'm not good enough for them. I keep thinking that maybe if I had more money, a better status, they'd at least try to understand.

I'm sorry that I even tied you up in all of this. I don't regret falling in love with you one bit, but I am sorry that I'm a boy, and that that's not okay with your mum and dad. I feel partly to blame for that, in more ways than one.

And I'm sorry that this is happening to you. That

you feel like you have to hide who you are from the world. I know I can never put myself in your shoes, that all of us in this magical land have such different experiences and families and identities, but I'm sorry that yours isn't easy.

I'm sorry that I can't help. I wish I could. I wish that more than anything.

If you ever need a place to stay, I have a small house and sleep on a bunk bed, but we have a sofa you could kip on, and I know jobs you could do, skilled jobs, jobs you'd easily get.

Don't shut me out.

Lots of love and extra chocolate sprinkles,
        Patrick xxx

TEN

Abe was silent on the ride home, sat in the back of a large cab with his parents and Lottie. He couldn't catch their eyes for fear of glaring, so he stared at his hands, burning a hole through his palm with the intensity of it all.

How *dare* his parents make him choose like that? If it had been a girl he'd stayed away with, there'd be no issue. Maybe the fact they weren't married, though he was sure his parents would sort that soon enough.

But it was Patrick, and Patrick was a boy.

He wasn't sure if it was simply the lack of grandchildren that bothered Mr and Mrs Cane, or whether their staunch old-fashioned ways held the most issues. There was no opportunity to adopt or use a surrogate mother, like humans did - it wasn't the elf way of doing things. They knew full well that if Abe was gay, the shop would die with him.

And yet thinking of life without the shoe business… Abe had no idea what it would entail. All his fancy schooling had built up to one thing: running his father's shop. He had no alternative, no ulterior passions up his sleeve. The only things in life he'd ever truly cared about were his future and Patrick, and now that he had to choose between the two, he had no idea which way to turn.

After being dropped off at his apartment block, he invited Lottie up to his flat on the top floor. They didn't speak as they climbed the stairs, Abe striding ahead, taking two steps at a time, while Lottie hung back. He pushed the key into the lock and shoved through the door, holding it bluntly open for her as she stepped inside.

"Drink?" he asked, kicking his bag across the floor.

"I'll have an eggnog," she replied, and he dipped inside the fridge begrudgingly to pour her a glass.

Perching on two ends of the sofa, Abe and Lottie watched each other warily, unsure of who should speak first. They both tried at once, meeting in a tangle of awkward conversation starters and retracting immediately, cheeks bright red and hands clutching shaking glasses.

"I'm sorry, Abe," Lottie began again, pulling her best apologetic face. "I didn't tell your parents you were with Patrick, but they knew what was going on when they realised you'd lied about going with me. I tried to stop them from meeting you at the station, but –"

"Yeah." Abe put up a hand to stop her. "It's okay, Lotts, I know what they're like."

The room dissolved into silence again.

"I just…" He glanced down at his drink and swilled it round, the sloshing sound echoing around the room. "I just don't know what to do, Lottie. The business is my whole future. But Patrick…"

"You love him?" Lottie asked. She was watching him with a curious expression, pointed ears stood up straight and button nose quivering.

"I love him."

"Well then you have to do the right thing." Lottie stood up, and held out a hand for her best friend to grasp. "Come on, Abe. You've got to at least *try*. There's no point running the shop and taking on this amazing, ready-made future if you'll never truly be happy."

"But how do I *know* what happiness is?" he queried, glancing back up at her, blue eyes filling with tears. "One false move now, and I'm tipping my entire future down the drain."

He didn't really mean that, though. That weekend, he'd experienced true happiness for the first time in his life. *That* was what he needed to hold onto. The feeling of Patrick's bare skin, soft against his; hot lips against the side of his neck, shifting down his body; cold snow and a vibrant blue sky, bursting above them amid icy clouds and jagged trees.

He wanted Patrick. Every ounce of his body *craved* him. At twenty years of age, he'd truly thought his time had gone, that he'd never experience such feelings of love and desire.

Yet now that he had, he was contemplating throwing them away.

"You know what happiness is, Abe," Lottie replied. "You've got to search inside yourself to find it."

***

It was late afternoon now, but Lottie led Abe out into the street on eager feet.

"Come on, Abraham! If you want to meet Patrick before he goes to work, we'll have to be quick."

"Or we could meet him on Tinsel Street," Abe suggested. "Instead of walking all the way to the Natale Region…"

"But romantic gestures, Abe, romantic gestures!"

They walked in a bubble of feverish anticipation, heartrates high. The air was frozen solid and brought a chill to their skin, noses and ears turned red, eyelids turned purple-pink, as bitter fog nipped at their faces. The last few elves wandered home from work or days out shopping, with bags containing carefully picked Christmas gifts and food for their Sunday roast; one elf was clutching a large ham as he scurried down the street towards them, teeth gritted and scarf wrapped tight against the cold.

"Evening!" he called, passing Lottie and Abe in his haste. That was another thing about the North Pole. Everyone was polite and would greet even the vaguest of strangers with a wave of their hand or a quick, "Hello!"

"Change of plan," Lottie said suddenly, as they neared a junction. "There's no way we'll make the Natale Region in time, Abe. We're gonna have to hit Tinsel Street!"

"What did I tell you…" Abe rolled his eyes, but his heart was spinning even faster now, alive with the knowledge that he'd be seeing Patrick even sooner than expected.

"Have you planned what you're going to say?" she asked, cutting through his thoughts. "If you want this to be successful, you can't just say you've picked him. You need something cute!"

"I don't think Patrick will –"

"Oh, trust me. He looks like the kind of guy who *loves* a grand gesture." Lottie's eyebrows were creased in the middle, as she poked him playfully on the arm. "Come on, then – what happened this weekend?"

"I don't know what you mean," Abe replied, though his cheeks were tinged with pink and Lottie rolled her eyes at his weak defence.

"A weekend away in a cottage on a mountainside, no parents in sight, and you're telling me *nothing* happened?"

"Well…" Abe shrugged, eyeing her warily. "Nothing you

need to worry yourself about, anyhow."

"So something *did* happen?" she asked, bouncing up and down as they walked, dodging a group of younger elves on skateboards and scooters. "Oh, come on, Abe, you have to tell me!"

"We…" But Tinsel Street was looming on the horizon, and Abe could hardly find the words to reply.

As they turned down the familiar cobbled street, Abe's heart was in his mouth and his hands were shaking. A brass band played on at the corner, blasting 'In the Bleak Midwinter' as a very apt description of the current weather, collecting donations in a violin case for orphaned elves. Stalls sold candy cane hot chocolate, magical gas lamps and warm mince pies, fresh from the oven, and elves everywhere rushed back and forth in their winter attire, searching high and low for the right gifts.

"How lucky he is to work here!" Lottie exclaimed, tugging on Abe's hand. "He really *is* perfect, Abe. He doesn't happen to have any single friends, does he?"

"Just David, and he's an absolute prick."

The café was open, the door propped behind a wooden carving of Santa, menu stood in the cold air beside it. Patrick told Abe he started work at five and had a two hour shift, so he wasn't due to arrive for another half hour or so, and Lottie was through the door and at the counter before he could hold her back.

"An Irish cream hot chocolate, please," she asked, smiling and holding out a handful of coins. "Abe, what would you like?"

"That's not gonna cover two drinks, love," the waitress replied, pushing Lottie's hand away. "This is a decent café, not a takeaway outlet. It's ten coins per drink."

Eyes wide, Lottie turned to Abe. "You… you don't happen to have any more money, do you, Abe?" Turning back to the waitress, she gulped and retracted her hand, waiting for Abe to tinkle coins onto it.

They made their way to the corner of the room with their mugs, were they sat on sofa-style seats with their backs to the window. Abe had chosen the same candy cane flavour he'd been served last time, but it didn't taste the same without Patrick's special touch. They drank in silence, one eye glued to the door, Abe's leg moving up and down rapidly as they waited.

"You okay?" Lottie asked, placing a hand on his knee to steady it. "Come on, Abe, you don't want to be a nervous wreck when Patrick arrives, do you?"

At that very moment, footsteps sounded on the doorstep, and Abe turned around hurriedly to…

"Abe!"

Patrick was stood in the doorway, all red cheeks and puffy eyes, flanked by Dora and David. He already had his navy apron tied around his stomach, and was wearing that familiar grey hoody and coat with its fluffy hood, looking exactly like the oversized teddy bear Abe had come to love so much.

"Patrick," he replied, cheeks flushing pink as they stared at each other. "I… this is Lottie."

With a quick hop and a wide, white-toothed smile, Lottie was up and away from the table. She held out a hand to shake Patrick's, before turning to Dora and David.

"It's lovely to meet you," she said politely. "How about we go and sit down while the boys talk?"

With that, she jerked Abe up and off the sofa, pushing him towards Patrick and out of the door.

Now trapped in the cold air, the boys were nervous again,

unsure of what to say. It wasn't usually like this, never so awkward or nerve-wracking, and it didn't seem real that just less than twenty-four hours ago, they'd slept together in a heavy four-poster, naked bodies pressed together between extravagant sheets. Abe couldn't even look at Patrick properly, not now that he'd seen him like that; he couldn't shake the image from his mind.

Eventually, he cleared his throat and turned to him, attempting a smile.

"So... I'm sorry about my parents." He tried to put on a light, airy voice, but it wavered dramatically and he was forced to cough again. "They're very traditional, see."

"It's okay." Patrick gave him a small smile back. "It's not your fault, Abe. We're just from very different places, me and you. You're a Noël boy, I'm a Natale boy. Maybe that's why our kinds don't mix."

"I suppose, but... there's more to me than where I was born," Abe said. "My parents can't control me forever, and I don't want to let them."

"What are you saying?" Patrick asked, frowning. "That you don't want the business after all?"

"I'm saying that I'd rather follow my heart and happiness than spend the rest of my life doing something I'm not passionate about, just because it's easy." He swallowed, then reached out to grasp Patrick's hand, finally looking up to meet his eyes. "I want to be with you, Patrick. You're the only thing that's ever made me truly happy, and I –"

"No," Patrick cut in, shaking his head. "You don't mean that, Abe. It's only because I'm your first, only because you've never felt like this before…"

"But I know I'll never feel like this again," Abe finished. "You're it for me. I love you, you know I do."

"And I love *you*," Patrick echoed. "And that's why I can't let you do this, Abe. You have your whole future set out for you, an amazing opportunity to be rich and comfortable and successful. You don't want to be tied to me, some poor boy from the Natale Region. You *know* you don't."

Abe's lips were trembling, but he tried to cut in still, holding up a hand to interrupt. "You don't understand! I don't care about the business, it's not important to me –"

"Not now, no. But one day, you'd turn around and think about all you'd thrown away, and understand what I mean."

"I wouldn't, Patrick, you know I wouldn't. I just want to be with you –"

"I'm sorry, Abe." There were tears in Patrick's eyes as he turned away, shaking his head. "I'm so, so sorry."

Dear Patrick,

Another letter I'll never send. Words I'll never find the courage to post in that little red box. A waste of ink, maybe. But where else can I pour my words, if not to you? I've never been as vulnerable, as honest, with someone as I was with you. You changed my whole life, Patrick.

I still can't quite bear to think it might actually be... over.

If I were a braver elf, a stronger elf, I'd send you this letter. I'd beg for you to take me back. I'd tell the truth... the truth being that I love you, that I know my future should be your future too, that in choosing my father and the business I'm choosing the easy way out. I'm a coward, and I'm embarrassed to admit that I am.

But I'm not a brave elf, a strong elf. I'm a failure. I can't believe I found love, real, pure love, and allowed you to rip it from me, on Tinsel Street, like you knew I wouldn't fight back, wouldn't even try to prove you wrong.

Does that make me a bad elf, a bad guy?

Do you hate me?

When I was thirteen, lonely, closeted, insecure, I used to dream about elves like you. Elves who were happy and content and comfortable. Elves who weren't afraid. I used to close my eyes and wish upon a star that one day, I'd either be you, or be with you.

I know now that I want both.

I'm sat in my apartment now, and the light is on. I'm cold. I think I've always been cold. The sun has set and there's a crescent moon out, and I'm thinking of that night in the cottage, the moon shining through the window, a perfect half, glowing midnight in the dark. I was brave, in that moment. I think you made me braver, braver than I'll ever be.

This is my fight, Patrick. I wish I had the courage to just take the risk.

All my love,

    Abe x

ELEVEN

For a second, Abe stood there, staring at the pavement. Was he dreaming?

Patrick had disappeared inside but the street was alive with shoppers, bustling here and there with their electric grins and pointed ears all aglow with Christmas cheer. It was Tinsel Street, where memories were made and hopes made true, but all Abe felt were tinsel *tears*, rolling down his cheeks, scratchy, sore. He'd never felt so lonely. It was an unfamiliar feeling, especially for Abe. It was almost as if he were the only elf in the whole entire world.

Had that really happened? He *must* be dreaming.

Patrick loved him. He wouldn't just…

But he had. Despite everything, Patrick had dropped him as quickly as he'd found him. Was he really that easy to abandon? Gone was that longing, brown-eyed expression, puppy-dog eyes staring into his own. Cold cobbles stared back at him from the floor, slush-ridden and mournful in the weak lamplight.

"Abe!" came a cry from the doorway. Lottie ran out and threw her arms around him, a tiny whirlwind of brown curls and fiercely pink cheeks. Her chin jutted into his shirt and left an imprint of smudgy green eyeshadow. It sparkled in the lamplight.

"Are you okay?" she asked, trying to peer into his eyes, his face. "Patrick just told us what happened, and I can't believe he'd... Abe? Oh my *baubles*, Abe, please speak to me!"

But Abe couldn't speak, the words stuck behind a lump in his throat.

"Abe, let's get you home. We needn't stay now. Come on, *please*. I'll pay for a cab."

His feet were stuck to the pavement, weighed down by a heavy heart. He didn't even want to move them. His thoughts were frozen solid, too, stuck on the memory of Patrick, the speech, spinning through his mind at six thousand miles per hour.

Tinsel Street was still alive with shoppers and music, the scent of warm cookies and hot chocolate drifting between them like a thin line of bedraggled smoke. Elderly couples strolled arm in arm, smiling, laughing, as their grandchildren skipped ahead with little brown bags of candied fruit and nuts. Teens danced in rows smoking cinnamon-infused cigarettes; they were trying to look cool, hopping around in sneakers imported from America and branded hoodies of gold and blue. The street moved around them, round, round, round, as if there was nothing wrong, like the world wasn't completely over, like things were *absolutely fine*.

Abe didn't notice the tears rolling down his cheeks until Lottie's arm was around him, squeezing tight.

"Come on, Abe. It's freezing out here."

She paid for a cab for the two of them. It pulled up at the end of Tinsel Street with a great black horse and a headpiece of giant feather plumes, kicking sleet with perfect hooves, but Abe was in another world. This driver wasn't half as nice as the one in the Jul Region. He grunted as they climbed onto the seat, rolling his eyes at Abe's puffy face and running nose.

"Where to?" he asked, grunting again as Lottie told him the name of Abe's block, beginning to slowly trot away from the curb.

She promised to stay the night, but Abe could hardly register what she was saying. He didn't care who was there or who wasn't there, if that person wasn't Patrick; nothing else mattered. As they approached the apartment block, Abe swaying like a drunk and Lottie holding him steady, he felt ready to collapse and stay down forever. What other end was he destined for?

He never thought he'd fall in love this Christmas… but he never expected to feel pain like this, either, didn't know of his *capability* to. Gnawing, inconceivable pain, tearing at his soul with never-ending claws and scraping at his mind. It didn't make a difference if he shook his head hard enough or reached to punch the walls, the sofa, the glossy dining room table his parents had forked out for…

Nothing, not one thing, eased his feelings. Breaking the lavish apartment was one thing, but it hardly mattered if he didn't have Patrick.

Why did people bother falling in love, if this was how it ended? Why go through the fun, the kisses, the deep conversations… if all it did was build up to one huge tangle of feelings, feelings which ripped you into a thousand pieces, each equally as painful to bear?

The deeper and faster you fall, the more it hurts when you hit the ground.

That's how it works, right?

Perhaps it was better like this, after all. Because if he didn't risk being hurt like this again, he could live the rest of his life in peace. Maybe he could find an elf to bear his children, live a life free of pain and anguish. That would be nice.

But that wasn't how he really felt.

He *loved* Patrick. Despite having only properly known him a week, he knew that Patrick loved him too. Maybe in Patrick's world, it would all be easy. His family were accepting of his sexuality; no one would've minded if he couldn't have children, if he didn't follow tradition.

But he wasn't from Patrick's world. That was the whole point.

He was from the Noël Region, and if he couldn't have kids to carry on his family's business, he was no good to anyone.

Maybe it wasn't so black and white, so bleak.

But that was how he felt.

"Here," Lottie said, appearing beside him with a glass of eggnog and a gingerbread man. "You need something in you, Abe." She winced at her poor choice of words, like Abe had even noticed, and added, "Not… you know what I mean."

Perching beside him on the sofa, she forced the glass into his shaking hand and helped him carefully lift it to his lips. A drop dribbled down his chin and onto his shirt, which she wiped away with a tissue, before curling an arm round his back and resting her head on his shoulder.

"Oh, Abe. We really are in a pickle, aren't we?"

"Oh, Lotts," he murmured, the smile on his face small but inevitable.

"Did you… did you *do it*?" It was a tactless question, but Lottie's face was innocent and open, like she didn't understand the gravity of her words.

"Yeah," Abe said. "Last night."

They were silent for a moment, the air of the apartment dense and muggy, like fog between them. Abe couldn't stop his knee from jiggling up and down again, a welcome distraction from the pain.

"I wish I hadn't done it," he added suddenly. "You think it's a good idea at the time, but then after… I don't know. It's made things so much harder, Lotts."

"I get it," she said, nodding wisely. "It must *suck*, Abe."

"It does."

Then he stood up, swinging his fists violently, and crossed over to stand in the centre of the room. "You know why it sucks, Lottie? Because I like guys, not girls. I can't just meet someone and fall in love, just like that, not when I'm… me. Even when I do finally meet a guy, it doesn't work out. There's always some obstacle, something that gets in the way of me just being *happy*. It doesn't matter if it's my parents, traditions, the business… I don't know. There's always one little thing that means I can't be normal, and I'm *sick* of it."

There were tears in his eyes as he turned to face her again, shaking his head and swallowing hard, trying to dissolve the still-growing lump in his throat. "What's wrong with me, Lottie? Why do I have to be like this? I've never been like the other boys – or even the other girls. I've always felt different, looked different. I'm abnormal. That's what my parents think, I know they do."

"There's nothing wrong with you!" Lottie exclaimed. "You're my amazing, talented friend, and Patrick clearly thinks that too."

"But he doesn't, does he? Because he's not fucking *here*, Lottie. He probably just used the whole business thing as an excuse to not be with me anymore, to soften the blow, you know. It wouldn't surprise me. Who would love a freak like me?"

He paused, then added softly, "I'm a failure of a son. I

have one friend, as awesome as you are, Lotts. I was a twenty-year-old closeted virgin until last night, and if I wasn't going into the shoe business, I'd have no skills, no interests, nothing but an education and… and… I'm useless, Lotts. I'm pathetic."

"You *know* that's not why Patrick ended things, Abe. He wanted what's best for you." Lottie frowned, cocking her head to one side. "You know… maybe it's not the worst thing in the world. There'll be someone else, once you have the business and you're set up for the future. Maybe someone they can approve of, a guy from Noël. Your parents couldn't stop you. Not if he had money, too…"

"It'll be a partnership up until Dad dies," Abe interjected. "And I'm not wishing death on my *dad*, Lotts. They're expecting me to have a wife or kids, or I don't get the shop. That's it."

"Then maybe… maybe…"

"I'll fall in love with a woman?" He laughed bitterly. "What good is love anyway? All I need is a *wife*, apparently. It doesn't matter that I love guys, because they're not looking for *feelings*. Children. Elves to carry on the Cane name. Why didn't *they* have more children, eh? Instead of pinning all their hopes on me!"

"I… I'd marry you, Abe. We could pretend we couldn't have children, and date other people in the meantime. We wouldn't have to –"

"They'd *know*, Lotts! They'd know!"

"I guess." Lottie squirmed, before standing up to go over to him. "Oh, Abe. I don't know what else to say."

"Then don't say anything," he replied, then shook his head and sighed, glancing at her apologetically. "No, I'm sorry, I didn't mean to snap. You're helping, Lotts, just by… well, by being here, I guess."

"That's what friends are for," she replied, nestling into him. "I love you, Abe. You know that, right?"

Abe nodded, attempting a smile back.

"Yeah," he said. "I do."

He paused, and Lottie looked at him inquisitively, like her own heart was breaking for the both of them.

"I love you, too, Lotts."

Dear Abe,

I'm sorry.

Is that all I have to say to you, now? That I'm sorry, and that I'm a messed-up excuse of an elf? Clearly. Because if I had more to say, I'd put a time and a place on the back of this letter - and a stamp - and say all of this to you in person.

Am I doing the right thing? That's maybe the hardest part of breaking up with someone. Wondering, always, if this could've been it. The One. The One you read about in books and see in movies, all that soulmate stuff. I want to believe it, Abe. I really do.

If I were you, maybe I'd feel differently. But I'm not you. I'm from the Natale Region. I don't have opportunities. I don't have hopes, dreams. I can't. We can't.

And so I can't let you throw away your future, because you don't understand how precious it is.

One day, I hope you do, too.

Lots of love and sprinkles,
        Patrick xxx

TWELVE

Love is a complicated feat, not least when you're twenty and experiencing the sensation for the first time, wrapped up in the vibrant colours it throws at you, trying to dodge the pain between sharp blows of ecstasy. You *think* you know best, in those moments. You think your decision is final, that everything you do and say is for the best.

That's certainly what Patrick thought that night, returning into the café with an expression set like stone and a throat full of jagged tears, like the fragments of tinsel lining the street. David, Dora and Lottie were sat around the table, laughing and sharing hot chocolates, a plate of untouched cookies set before them. They were silent as he approached, watching him with wide eyes and anger-infused expressions.

"You did it, didn't you?" Dora said first. "Oh, Patrick, *please* tell me you didn't!"

Patrick sat down opposite without saying a word, moving his hands together on his lap and flicking his wrists. The jolts of pain did wonders in disguising the larger jolts his heart was facing. Then he swallowed, before glancing up to meet her eyes.

"I told him he should take the business."

Dora and David proceeded to turn and stare at each other,

disbelieving, as Lottie sprang from the table and rushed outside. Patrick's face was hot.

After a moment of pause, Dora turned back to him, shaking her head.

"No," she said, voice an octave higher than usual. "You wouldn't *do that*, Patrick. You love Abe. He was going to choose *you*. Why would you tell him to take the business if that's not what he wants?"

"Because I'm not stupid," he replied. "I know what's best for him. I know he'd only come to regret it in time."

"You don't know that at all!" Dora tried to interject, but Patrick put up a hand to stop her.

"I've only known him a week, Dora. That's not enough time to let him jeopardise his future for me. I'd be selfish if I let him."

"But it's not *just* a week," she argued, while he cocked his head in confusion. "Yes, it's a week *physically*, in real time, but it's been so much more than that for both of you. The Patrick I know doesn't just sleep with guys on a whim. You're not like that. You'd only do that if you loved and trusted the person, and by the sound of it, Abe is the same. Patrick, you invited this guy for a weekend away in your grandparents' cottage, and you're telling me you *don't* want to be with him? If you genuinely think you're doing the right thing, I don't know you at all."

Patrick didn't know what to say. He twisted his hands together and frowned, still staring down at the table with impenetrable intensity.

"You're in *love* with each other, and you've thrown it away just because you think you're being sensible. When did anyone get anywhere being *sensible*?" Dora turned to David, poking a finger at his arm. "Come on, David. Back me up!"

"I do think it's rather stupid, Pat," David agreed. "Not your finest move."

"Exactly." Dora scowled, triumphant. "And *he's* supposed to be the sensible one!"

Patrick swallowed, still moving his hands together on his lap in an attempt to distract himself. But now, with bile rising in his throat and his heartrate clunking higher and higher, he felt sick.

He *had* made the right decision... hadn't he?

He started his shift with David at five, grateful for something to take his mind off the pain. He made endless hot chocolates, made small talk with customers, threw batch upon batch of cookies into the stove and burnt at least three. Each candy cane hot chocolate stung his heart, each round of camembert a stark reminder of their weekend away. It was all too hot and painful in his mind. He pressed too much garlic into the cuts, added too much peppermint extract to the hot chocolate, almost cried right into a croissant before David handed him a tissue.

"You're not yourself tonight, Patrick," the floor manager said, bustling past him to collect a pile of dirty plates from the counter. "It's not something to do with all that drama you kids were having earlier, is it? If so, there's a time and a place, and our café is neither."

"Sorry, Ma'am," Patrick apologised, through gritted teeth. "I didn't realise the breakup would be such an inconvenience."

"The breakup? Oh, Patrick, I'm so sorry. You should've said earlier, you fool. I'd have let you take the night off."

"It's fine," he replied, though the lump in his throat had doubled upon saying the word out loud. "I'm fine."

He walked home with Dora and David on either side of

him, arms linked as they made their way back to the Natale Region. It was a long journey, but paying for a cab would burn through their wages, and the streets were silent and frosty, almost completely empty. Sunday roasts wafted through windows, and smoke rose from the windows of those who could afford a fire. In the Noël Region, practically every other house was lit up for Christmas in some way; yet as they approached their own part of town, the chimney breasts and fairy lights vanished, giving birth to rows of grey-black terraced houses with paper decorations sodden from the snow, flaking front doors painted each colour of the rainbow.

The street vendors had shut up for the night, but the scent of spices and frying onions was still alive in the air, drifting beneath their noses. Homeless elves lay in doorways and across benches in cab shelters, tucked under wasted wrapping paper and dregs of brown paper. One was licking the inside of a food carton with a long, dry tongue, trying to retrieve the last dregs of nourishment to feed his bawling stomach. Once upon a time, it might've signified in Patrick's mind that he'd done the right thing, that Abe was lucky to have the privilege and luxury his family provided.

But now, he was starting to wonder what difference it actually made to the rest of the North Pole.

"Would you like us to stay over?" Dora asked, squeezing Patrick's arm tight. "We don't mind, you know."

"No, it's okay. You two get home. I'll be fine."

His door was at the end of the street, beside the gates of a large doll factory. The smoke was splattered across their own windows and turned the water in their pipes a murky grey-brown colour, but it had provided his mother's employment almost all her life. He pushed through the smog and tried his hardest not to breathe in, then slammed the door shut behind him, sagging to the floor.

"Ma, Patrick's home!" came a small voice. Before he could straighten up, a tiny body had latched onto his, all claws and huge eyes and messy hair.

"Hey, Betsy," he murmured, rubbing his sister's head. "Do you mind detaching yourself from Patrick?"

"No," she crowed delightedly, grinning up at him with a toothless mouth. "Come and play Monopoly, Patrick! I need you on my team, because Stevie keeps cheating…"

The family room was small and cramped, and the three kids were sat with his mother, crouching on the decaying dining room table they'd inherited some years ago. Their old-fashioned British Monopoly board and most of the cards had been donated years ago by a Noël charity fighting to help poverty-stricken children in the Natale, Navidad and Weihnachten Regions, but they were still searching for Park Lane and Piccadilly, both of which were missing in the box.

"Good weekend, love?" his mum asked, smiling and beckoning him over. "It was quiet without you around the house. Give us a kiss!"

Trying to force a cheerful expression, he bent to kiss his mother on the cheek. "It was great, Ma," he replied. "Just great."

"Did you get much snow?" she asked, while Betsy tugged on his hand, pulling him onto a seat beside her. He sat down and began to flick through her cards, smiling as her warm body nestled against him, all fragile limbs and sickly skin, feet pressed against his thigh like ice blocks.

"It snowed a lot when we first got there," he replied. "Then it calmed down overnight."

"And the boy you went with?" His mother winked as she said this, trying not to catch his eye. "He had a good time, too? I assume we'll be allowed to meet him soon, if you don't think we're too embarrassing…"

"It didn't work out, actually." The room fell silent, even his little brothers and sisters staring up at him solemnly. "Yeah. It just wasn't meant to be."

They played the rest of the game quietly, Stevie still cheating and the rest of the family too subdued to mention it. Nine-year-old Betsy, the youngest of the clan, fell asleep against him with her thumb firmly in her mouth, and the twins at the other end of the table finished a box of chocolates incognito. The heating wasn't on – they'd run out of coins, apparently – so they sat around a tiny candle, trying to gather warm from the flickering flame.

Patrick's family might not have much money, but they certainly rich in their love for one another.

They played until it was time for bed, when his mum promised to make them all hot chocolates and bring them upstairs with her. Patrick helped, not commenting on the meagre amounts she spooned from out-of-date packaging, filling the cups three-quarters water and the rest milk, pushing the mugs near to the kitchen stove in an attempt to salvage some heat. She stirred each with a single spoon, watching the chocolate finally dissolve.

"It might not be as nice as that café of yours makes it, but it's something different." She picked three up with one hand, gesturing for Patrick to grab the other two before pushing open the door.

Following behind her, Patrick said eventually, "You'll have to come down sometime, let me make you a drink." He paused as she began to protest, adding, "My Christmas present, to you."

His mother turned to glance properly at him, then.

"Thank you, Patrick," she said. "That would actually be... well, very nice."

They tucked the kids into bed with their hot chocolates, plumping the pillows for the twins on the floor and patting Betsy's sheets against the sides of the narrow camp bed she inhabited. Stevie slept on the bottom bunk and had almost conked out anyway, no doubt dreaming of the bike he wanted for Christmas; Patrick slept on top. He climbed the steps to his own mattress with his drink carried precariously in one hand, ready to spill.

"Careful, Pat!" his mum warned. "I won't be washing the sheets tonight if you get chocolate all over them."

Nestling into his pillow with his head against the window, he watched the kids waving from beneath the covers and grinning as they were tucked away, pointed ears shining in the dim light, shivering, trying not to show it. His mother shut the door with a click, and the room was submerged in darkness. It was silent now, aside from Stevie's heavy breathing and Betsy's sniffles. Lying here, head against the wall and heart thumping beneath his chest, Patrick had never felt such love pulsing through him; warmth, a feeling of belonging, of desire to protect his family at all costs.

Maybe Dora and David were right, and love was what *truly* mattered. Who cared if he and Abe weren't suited for one another, or if Abe's family disapproved? Who cared if Abe wouldn't inherit the business he had no passion for? Who cared if things might go wrong, and life lead them down different points in the future? He *loved* Abe. He'd never been so certain about something in his whole entire life.

And if you truly love something, you *have* to fight for it.

Dear Patrick,

I've slept since we last saw each other. Strangely, my heart feels just as attached. It hurts, and so do my eyes, which well up just at the thought of you. And yet my brain is slowly starting to come around to the idea that maybe… maybe you were never meant to be it for me.

That's a really hard realisation to bear.

When I thought of the future, it always felt kind of blurry. You put it into 3D, 4D, whichever one you can touch and smell and kiss.

My heart still wants you back, but my head knows that isn't possible. Maybe you were right, and I was too naïve to see it. Maybe we were too young, and it happened too fast. Maybe it wasn't meant to be.

I hope you're keeping well.

All my love,

                Abe x

THIRTEEN

"You *have* to go to the ball," Lottie said, throwing down her hat in fury. "Abe, it's *Santa's Christmas Ball*! You can't just *not go*. That's not an option here."

They were stood in the town's most extravagant dress shop, testing fabrics and hats and ribbons. Hidden behind a rack of voluptuous silk hats adorned with wintry flowers and trim, Lottie turned to Abe, hands on hips and curls strung into an elaborately messy bun.

"I don't want to go, Lotts," Abe reasoned. He picked up the hat she'd thrown down and proceeded to straighten out the ribbon and trim, tweaking the collection of holly berries sewn onto the rim. "I don't feel like dancing and dressing up and eating posh food. I'd rather just stay home and eat sour cream snowballs in bed."

Shaking her head, Lottie flicked him heavily on the arm. "You're going to the ball, Abe. We're buying a suit, then, next weekend, we're *going to the ball*."

"Why?" he asked, swivelling round so as not to face her. "I'd rather not bother. I just…"

"Look." Grabbing his hand and tugging him back to her, Lottie cocked her head and frowned. "You've been moping around all week like it's the end of the world, and, as your best friend, it's *my* job to get you out of that state. Do you not *want* to be happy, Abe? Do you not want to go back to the way you were before?"

Sighing, Abe rolled his eyes. Lottie didn't get it. He hadn't been happy before, not at all. He'd merely… existed. Existed for his family, for Lottie and the future he had laid out before him. It hadn't been enjoyable; nor had it meant anything to him.

Until Patrick, he hadn't even understood the *meaning* of true happiness.

Yet Lottie was gazing at him with such a beseeching, brown-eyed gaze that he couldn't say no.

"Fine," he frowned, pushing the hat back on her head. "Let's find you a dress."

They paraded the shop with eyes on stalks, examining closely every length of fabric, every line of silk, every button and bead and sparkling thread. The dresses were mostly made on demand, custom to each lady and her needs, but Lottie wanted it to be perfect; she needed each element of the dress to be expertly chosen and matching, combined to create one fabulous outfit.

"I *need* to find a husband this year," she said, plucking at a line of violet silk. "It's all my parents go on about, Abe. Ooh, isn't this a nice colour? It'd match my birthday earrings, don't you think?"

Abe had been best friends with Lottie for most of his life, and they'd gone dress shopping together every year since they were thirteen. He knew exactly what to say, each "it suits your figure" and "that's totally your colour" – even when the dress was bogey-yellow and clung to her in all the wrong places. He knew what she'd end up with, anyway; a strapless number with a modest neckline and a full skirt, reaching right down to the floor in a balloon.

She eventually went for the violet silk, softening it with pink-toned ribbons, strips of lace, pearls all the way up and down the back. It was beautiful, matching her pale complexion and glossy brown curls, and hugged her waist in just the right way. She spun around in the example dress in the changing room, holding up pearls and frills to see what looked best, muttering to herself and plucking at the fabric around her armpits and stomach with a frown.

It was expensive, of course, but neither batted an eyelash as they placed the order. The annual ball was always the most exclusive event of the year, and those invited could always afford to fork out for nice clothing. Only the most prestigious of elves and their children, once of age, were allowed to attend.

Held up high in Santa's castle – at the far end of the Noël Region, set amongst elaborate grounds – the ball was something the whole of the North Pole was heavily invested in. It was broadcast on the radio each household had, played out on speakers on street corners and in shops. It was even rumoured that some dressed up at home to pretend they'd been invited, and bought extraordinary food to mimic the Christmas feast.

"Done," Lottie said, holding her receipt in her hand and grinning. "I can pick that up next week, then I'm good to go. Shall we get you a suit, Abe?"

Abe nodded begrudgingly, and they both stepped out into the cold street. It was busier than usual, but then the Noël Region was *always* set alight before an event like this. Nail and hair salons, makeup counters, tailors, shoe shops and dressmakers had signs everywhere, advertising their services in glittery lettering. There were elves in raggedy clothing trying to sell their best suits, and security guards positioned to remove the beggars, accusing them of cluttering up the streets. They bought coffees at a stall and sipped them as they wandered up and down, trying to find the perfect tailors.

"I don't think you'll get a custom-made jacket at this short notice," Lottie said anxiously, tugging him to one side. "I had to get fitted months ago, and I booked a date to choose fabrics with the owner. It's a wonder I found one today, after it fell through. Do you think your parents will mind if we buy one that's a bit… cheaper?"

"If they do," Abe replied, through gritted teeth, "then I really don't give a toss."

Ever since his parents had made him choose between Patrick or the business, he'd been severely cold towards them. Having to see them was another reason he didn't particularly want to go to the ball.

They found a suit in no time, picking out black dress trousers in Abe's size, with a matching blue velvet jacket. The waistcoat was grey and the tie was red, but altogether, it somehow worked. With a sprig of holly in his pocket, Lottie decided he'd look almost… dapper.

"And it's not *that* cheap," she said, pulling a face as she examined the tag. "Don't tell anyone where you bought it, and you'll be fine!"

They took a cab home, sipping their coffees and talking amiably about the ball – about who would be there, what the feast would be like, what Mrs Claus would be wearing this year, how awful it was that Santa had taken ill, that his son Nick would be reading the speech. In some ways, it was almost nice to chat in such a casual, meaningless way, a way that took Abe's mind off Patrick for the first time in the last week.

And he *needed* to get over Patrick. He knew that. Patrick had made his decision not to be with him, and that was… fine. Well, it wasn't, but he couldn't do anything about it now.

It was just hard, moving on. Every inch of his body still craved for Patrick, for his soft brown hair and light coffee-coloured stomach, rolling over those fitted boxers…

"Abe?" Lottie cut in, dragging him back to reality. "You haven't been listening to a word I've been saying, have you?"

"Yes," he said, frowning and flushing. "You were saying…"

"That I hope Robin's going to be at the ball?" She let out an elaborate sigh and leaned back against the seat of the cab, pulling a face. "And that he better ask me out…"

"Have you ever even *spoken* to Robin before?" Abe asked, perhaps a little more curtly than he'd intended.

They arrived outside Abe's apartment block moments later, piling out of the cab and onto the cold street. The stairs stretched on above them, but they climbed in silence, a few steps apart. Reaching the top floor, Abe reached to push his key into the lock… when the door opened all by itself and he almost fell forward, the room expanding around him.

"Abe!" came a familiar voice, from inside the flat.

Grimacing, he straightened up and took a tentative step towards his parents.

Mr and Mrs Cane were perched on the sofa, drinking eggnog from his own glasses and eating sour cream snowballs from the stash above the stove. Trying not to glare, Abe walked forward, grabbing the packet from his mother's hands and faking the biggest, whitest smile he could muster.

"Mum!" he said. "Dad! What are you doing here?"

"Well…" Mrs Cane glanced sidewards at her husband,

then back to her son. "We heard you were going shopping for your suit today, and we wanted to come round and see it! We assumed you hadn't booked in advance. You won't have had it custom-made, will you?"

"No," Lottie piped up, from behind him. "It's nice to see you again, Mr and Mrs Cane! We managed to find a really, really nice suit for Abe. Not custom, but you can hardly tell."

"I'm sure it's lovely, Lottie," Mrs Cane sniffed. "Go and show us your suit, Abe. You can get changed in the bathroom, I'm sure."

Trying to keep a straight face and with his bag clutched tight in his hand, Abe crossed the floor and disappeared out of sight. Why did his parents have to make it seem like it was *their* house? Would they really never stop telling him what to do?

The bathroom was next to his bedroom; a tiny room with no window and LED lighting attached to the ceiling, the height of Arctic technology. He locked the door with a clunking nose and fell back against it, pure fury surging through his veins.

He didn't want to try on his stupid suit for his parents, any more than he wanted to wear it to the ball itself. He peeled off his chinos and shirt and folded them into a pile on top of the toilet, pulling the trousers over his pale, spindly legs, buttoning the waistcoat against his chest.

The jacket fit perfectly over his skinny frame, velvet blue against dark blond hair. It was warm, the perfect thickness against him, and drooped just over the tops of his thighs, masking the angle of his pelvis and knobbly knees.

Stepping back into the front room, he could feel it go silent around him.

"Oh, Abe!" His mother had tears in her eyes as she glanced

him up and down, shaking her head. "You look wonderful, darling."

Gerald was also a little choked up as he watched his son walk in front of them, a plastic smile tacked across Abe's face.

"She's right, son," Mr Cane said. "We're so, so proud of you. You really will blow everyone away."

"Thanks," Abe said, nodding awkwardly. Despite everything, he couldn't help but feel a twinge of nostalgia at their words; this was what he'd wanted all along, after all. For his parents to be proud of him, instead of despairing. "That… that means a lot."

Dear Abe,

I saw a newspaper article about Santa's Ball earlier, and thought of you. It's awful that Santa's ill, isn't it? His son Nick is a right prick, terrible hair. I find it so bizarre to think that you'll be there, in a fancy suit, eating all that good food. Think of me if they serve you a mince pie cocktail, won't you? Though I bet it won't be a patch on Dora's.

I'll be listening on the radio, of course. The kids love it, especially Betsy. Mum always lets her dress up in her favourite party dress (red sparkles and everything) and do her hair in a fancy bun, though Stevie thinks it's a waste of time and hates the food Mum tries to make for us. The twins don't have much time for Santa – or the aristocracy.

I wish you could've met them, you know. They're nothing like me, which is funny. I've always loved Santa. I mean, it would be cool to be him, sure, but I also think he just seems like a nice dude. Chilled, laid-back, you know? Anyway, I hope you have a good night.

Lots of love and sprinkles,
        Patrick xxx

FOURTEEN

The night of the ball came around sooner than expected, for it wasn't long until he was standing in his bedroom on the 21st of December, staring at his reflection in the mirror, all suited up and ready to go. He had holly berries dangling from the pocket of his velvet jacket, red socks peeking from above a pair of pointed brown brogues. As far as outfits went, he realised he'd smashed it; for although it might not be the most expensive, lavish suit he could've gone for, it was just so *Abe*.

He did his hair with far too much gel and hairspray, fighting to push the crazy bits into line. A dark blond quiff formed above his hairline and he smiled at his reflection, nodding. He looked… nice. Presentable and neat, like a frozen turkey, tucked and stuffed into the perfect shape.

Pushing his wallet into his pocket and straightening his tie, he stepped out into the hallway. His parents would be here any second, pulling up in a cab outside with Lottie and her parents. Mr and Mrs Arbre were the elf equivalent of human bankers and managed coins in a large building opposite the train station, sorting and counting and redistributing. They were pretty high up in that world, which was how they'd gotten to know Mr and Mrs Cane, hence their children being such good friends.

Lottie had always been pushed heavily by her parents to achieve. It wasn't until they told her, several years ago, that she was to go and work at the bank with them, that she realised her passion didn't lie beside theirs. She wanted to be a pâtissier, to make the finest French pastries in all of the Noël Region. She'd started an apprenticeship in a local bakery the summer before last, and Abe had never seen her so happy.

He poured himself a glass of Irish cream on ice as he waited, standing on the balcony with the cold liquid poised at his lips. Across from him, the river glowed yellow in the faded sunlight, the colour of tropical sands and perfect buttercream. He watched, a sigh held within him, as the world fell asleep and the sky clicked softly to black.

He wished, in that moment, that Patrick could see him like this, for just a second. That he could see his suit, his gelled hair, the impenetrable sadness within him… and maybe, *maybe*, it would make him change his mind.

But it wouldn't. He knew that. Patrick was gone. He hadn't chosen Abe.

What good was it trying to remember him?

The bell inside his apartment rang, alerting him that someone was downstairs. Downing the rest of his drink, he pushed his keys into his pocket and pulled the door shut behind him, hurrying down the steps two at a time to reach the lobby. Lottie was waiting for him by the door, lit by the lamplight.

"Oh, *Lotts*!" Abe gasped, eyes wide. "You look… just phenomenal!"

She was wearing her new purple dress, which flew out around her legs in a silky bubble and shimmied as she moved, brushing the floor. It was strapless, the rim of the dress pressing into her breasts and holding them tight, the perfect size and shape, and a pink ribbon held in her waist and round stomach. Despite it flowing around her, it showed her curvy figure perfectly, pearls shimmering across her back and below the ribbon's edge.

She'd done her hair in a bun, loose curls cascading over her shoulders and hanging in ringlets beside her face. Her brown eyes were lined with black and violet, lips the softest shade of glossy peach. Her cheeks and the tips of her pointed ears shone in the dim light of the lobby, and her face broke into the widest of grins as she saw Abe approaching her and lifted her arms to hug him.

"You look great, too," she whispered, right into his ear. He smiled, pulling back and glancing outside, to where a large cab was waiting for them, huge horses neighing and stamping their hooves impatiently.

"Shall we?" he asked, and she nodded and took his arm.

"We shall."

The air outside was frozen solid, for a chill hung deep around them and tickled their cheeks as they crossed the pavement to the cab. Abe helped Lottie up, offering her a hand before following after, taking a seat beside his parents. Mrs Cane was dressed in modest dark blue, no doubt not intending to match her son, and his father had a brown suit and candy cane striped tie, to honour their family name.

"You look lovely, Mum," Abe said politely, perching beside her as Lottie bunched up her skirts in order to fit opposite. "And you, Mrs Arbre!"

"Thank you, Abraham!" Lottie's mother beamed. "You two make a stunning pair, I must say! I'm always telling Lottie that, but she won't listen to me."

Mr and Mrs Cane jiggled in their seats as the two youths

tried to mask their laughter, snorting into hands and sleeves as Mrs Arbre glanced between them, bemused.

They set off into the night in the nick of time, travelling down the streets in their cab and gazing out the windows as the Noël Region drifted by, lit up by fairy lights and streetlamps, casting their world in a yellow glow and making puddles and snowdrifts sparkle. There were few people out on the streets, waving at the cabs as they went by, dressed in their own versions of ballgowns and suits as they threw rags and shouted at the cabs. They were vulgar, common cries that Mrs Cane had to turn away from, for fear their words would stain her dress.

Lottie and Abe were loving it, of course, and waved at the passers-by with regal hands. The castle was approaching in the distance, and as they left the houses behind and began up the long, winding drive which led to the front steps, Abe felt almost... *excited*.

It was rumoured that only those who were invited by Santa's own ink could access the road to the castle; if you weren't a guest, you'd be turned away the minute your feet hit the bricks. Only those with true intentions could reach the palace. It was always a huge privilege, something many an elf would never experience.

The castle was a huge, imposing building, built of beige stone and latticed windows, set beyond an elaborate fountain and curling drive. They pulled up in front of the steps and proceeded to climb out of the cab, thanking the driver as he pulled away from them. The procession of cabs moved steadily along the drive, couples dismounting, big smiles all around. They moved out the way quickly, clutching arms and mounting the steps.

"Abe!" Mrs Cane hissed, gesturing to Lottie. "Take her

arm!"

Lottie was smirking as they linked, nodding to each other and beginning to climb. The doors were open wide and the hall beyond was brightly lit, light shining against the polished black and white tiles and reflecting off the huge windows. Elves in their ballgowns and fancy suits paraded the place, waving and laughing and chattering.

The hall led into the ballroom through a pair of large, dark doors, trimmed with tinsel and candles. They lined up, arm in arm, to take the first steps into the party.

"Off you go, Abe," his mother muttered, nudging his foot. Clicking his heels together, he led Lottie forward, into the ball.

It was almost like someone had exploded Christmas in the middle of the ballroom. A display had been created by throwing lights, red, green and silver, across the walls and floor, in a collision of sparkles and colour. Tapestries lined the walls in all colours of the Yuletide, and tables lined the sides of the room, set with plates and goblets and cutlery, covered by a silver runner and masses of Christmas crackers. The floor was covered in pieces of papery fake snow, trampled on and spread about where feet had tread in tracks and prints. There was a new theme every year, twisting from colour to colour, tinsel to tears. This year, it was tradition, and Abe's eyes were all aglow.

"Oh, it's so beautiful!" Lottie breathed, eyes wide. "How *do* they do this every year?"

Shrugging, Abe tugged on Lottie's hand and pulled her forwards. He felt his shoulders drop. There was something comforting about the ball, something freeing and festive and lovely, which lessened the weight in his chest.

"There's the chocolate fountain!" he said, pointing to the

other side of the ballroom, a sparkle in his eye once again. "Come on, Lotts!"

Breaking free of their parents and hurrying across the dance floor, they were filled with bubbles of laughter and bright smiles, ducking between elaborate dresses and tightly suited elves, dodging couples and youths and teens with too many drawn-on freckles. The chocolate fountain had been left alone beside a large platter of mango, strawberries, marshmallows and stollen bites, and stared at them beseechingly, dripping gooey goodness. With wooden skewers they tucked in liberally, feeding each other with thick, chocolatey chunks of fruit and pudding, snorting as it dribbled down their chins and covered their teeth in sugary goodness.

Perhaps it wasn't the correct thing to be doing at Santa's Christmas Ball, but in the moment, it didn't seem to matter. Nobody was watching; they were too busy having fun of their own, laughing and stealing hors-d'œuvres, throwing their heads back so far that you could practically see their tonsils. Fancy dresses, hairstyles and jewellery were unnoticeable in a room full of many, and so they just laughed when chocolate landed on the silk of Lottie's skirt, rushing to wipe it clean.

Memories of Patrick were swallowed in that instant, for Abe was too happy to recall his sadness. A neighbour came over to shake his hand and dispatch season's greetings, complimenting him on his suit and fine lady, and he basked in the attention, the joy of it all.

"They think you're my girlfriend," Abe whispered, snorting. "I bet they're expecting a cheesy proposal, like Sally and Martin last year, over dessert. Maybe I should slip a ring into your Christmas pudding!"

But Lottie was elbowing him desperately, pulling a face of

distress. Clutching her skirts in one hand to hide the chocolate stain, she straightened up and spun around, announcing loudly, "Robin!"

Robin de Gui, Lottie's longstanding childhood crush, was stood before them in tight-fitting chinos and a pattered suit jacket, grinning lazily. He leaned forward to kiss Lottie on both cheeks in an incredibly European fashion, while she giggled and simpered and blushed bright pink.

"What a surprise!" she gushed, pulling back and wringing her hands together bashfully. "I thought you said you were over the ball this year?"

Robin frowned, cocking his head to one side. "When did I say that? I don't think we've spoken since high school."

"Oh." Lottie flushed an even deeper shade of pink, grasping at her skirts again. "I think I heard you say it to someone else, maybe…"

Abe cringed as Robin stepped past them, aiming for a skewer of mango, which he dipped into the melted chocolate fountain.

"I see," he replied, a little confused. "Well, it was nice seeing you both again. I hope you enjoy the rest of the ball." Then, taking a strawberry and two marshmallows and poking them under the sheet of molten cocoa, he turned and disappeared into the crowd.

With wide eyes and a face of pure horror, Lottie turned to Abe, hopping from foot to foot and clapping her hands ecstatically. "Did you see that, Abe? He came over to talk to us! He kissed me on *both cheeks*, Abe!"

Abe couldn't tell her that the only reason Robin had come over was to access the chocolate fountain, or that he'd since watched him proceed to cross the room with his chocolate skewers and pass them to a blonde girl, who fed them to him slowly and seductively, watching his teeth grab the marshmallow and tug it beneath his jaw. Lottie was so happy, bouncing about and shoving strawberries into her mouth, that he didn't want to hurt her.

The bell went for the start of the meal a couple of moments later, and they made their way carefully to their parents. Mrs Cane and Mrs Arbre were laughing as they took their seats, muttering under their breaths and pushing napkins into their bosoms. Their husbands were talking loudly about business, yet Mr Cane was watching his wife eagerly, trying to join the inevitably more interesting conversation.

"Evening." Abe grinned, taking his seat opposite them. "How are we all?"

The food materialised in front of them beneath silver cloches, a result of magic much stronger than of anywhere else in the North Pole. A prawn cocktail starter, tiny slivers hidden within a bed of rocket and slathered in pinky-red Marie Rose sauce, with olives and dips and breadsticks lined up in the middle of the table. Abe ate in silence as the ballroom bustled with laughter, trying not to think about the wonderful food he'd sampled inside the Gingerbread Restaurant with Patrick.

A fine roast made up their main course, bowls of potatoes, sprouts and glazed parsnips, along with monstrous Yorkshire puddings and sauces – bread sauce, horseradish, cranberry and mint. Each table had a whole roasted turkey, stuffing with sage and onion, a sprig of rosemary sticking out of its rear end. Peas, carrots, red cabbage and asparagus sat in dishes, dripping with hot butter and herbs. They ladled the food onto their plates with watering mouths and tucked in desperately, despite being stuffed from the hors-d'œuvres and starter.

"I could continue eating all evening!" Lottie said, biting down on a piece of asparagus as butter dripped down her wrist. "It's all just so good!"

The Christmas puddings were doused in brandy and set alight, identical blue flames flickering up and down the room. They were silent as this went on, eyes closed and heads down. In that moment, they were all at peace, minds together and hearts held tight.

In that moment, he wasn't thinking about Patrick.

In that moment, they were all, finally, free.

Dear Patrick,

I don't think I ever quite realised just how much Christmas is a time for the lonely. A time when splendour is exemplified beside abject poverty, beggars out in their throngs, children going without. Even in the North Pole, where we have so much, there are so many people wanting. How can that be?

I remember you making a comment about Nick, once, and you're right, you're so right. He's rich, so rich and greedy, and when he takes over from Santa, we'll all be in trouble. Santa is a good egg, though. Kind, genuine. A good leader. His yearly speech gives life to me, as I'm sure it does to you. Does that sound cheesy?

I have Santa's Ball soon, and while I'm so excited, I've never felt so lonely. This time of year is meant to be shared, but who do I have to share it with? Even Lottie's looking for love. I can't do that. I might never.

All my love,

              Abe x

FIFTEEN

As the plates were cleared and the sauces and dips removed from the tables, music began to play at one side of the room. Lively jazz exploded throughout the ballroom, loud and exhausting, and Abe couldn't help but grin as Lottie grabbed his hand and tugged him out of his chair.

"Come on!" she shouted. "Let's go dance!"

The dancefloor was full of heaving bodies and huge dresses, circling like brightly coloured spinning tops, jewels catching the light and glinting gold and silver. Neither of them had much experience dancing to jazz music, so they hopped up and down like bunnies at a disco, squealing with laughter as the music picked up and they raised their arms in the air, loving it, breathless...

Abe watched as a young elf slid up to them, someone he recognised from school – Simon, he thought – straightening his tie and bowing low. With one hand outstretched, he turned to Lottie and said, "May I have this dance?"

Spinning round to face Abe, she grinned, a smile wide enough to break her face in half. Taking the elf's hand, she turned back to him and nodded, allowing herself to be swallowed up by the ballroom.

Now alone on the dancefloor, Abe turned to try and spot

his parents. The crowd was too thick and the tables too far away, bodies everywhere and the air rife with sweat and laughter, too much jumping and jiving and laughing as the band played on. Slowly, one cautious move at a time, he began to dance; he moved his arms up and down, then swivelled his feet in a twist-like movement, wiggling his bum in time to the beat.

And, strangely enough, it was liberating. Dancing like nobody was watching gave him ownership of his thoughts and actions in a way it hadn't for so long, able to hop and shake and wobble across the tiles like he was the only person there, like nobody cared what he looked like.

He danced like a freak, he'd say if he were watching from the outside.

But he danced with heart, and really, that was all that mattered to him.

The music altered suddenly, spinning from fast, upbeat jazz to a slow, seductive tune. Groups and singletons began to back away to the side of the room, leaving space for couples, who bound their arms around each other and gazed into eyes as the tune slid on, romantic and gentle. Across the room, Abe spotted Lottie in the arms of the young elf, *Simon*, smiling placidly and staring forward, eyes like liquid gold.

Kiss him, he urged – and she did.

Seeing her there, like that, so *happy*, made him smile. She'd got what she wanted, and knowing she was experiencing something good and pure made his heart beam.

Moving slowly over to where his parents were sat, he felt a hand tap gently on his shoulder. Spinning, he came face to face with a beautiful elf, all long blonde hair and pale skin, eyes bright blue in the light of the ballroom.

"Would you like to dance?" she asked, nervous, in a high,

feminine voice.

Abe turned back to where his parents were sitting, next to Mr and Mrs Arbre. They were watching him with narrowed eyes, waiting for his response, begging him to say yes.

"Sure," he said, a little stilted, before allowing her to tug him onto the dancefloor.

The lighting had dimmed, to the point of being almost intimate, and the elf slid sensual hands over his shoulders and behind his neck as they shuffled up close. Abe wasn't sure where to place his own hands, so plumped for her waist, fixing them just above her slim hips. Her dress was backless and so he tried to avoid his fingers meeting her bare skin, his actions awkward, stilted.

They moved around the dancefloor at the same pace as the other couples, feet and toes twisting as they switched places, spinning around. The elf had her eyes fixed on his face. Abe couldn't avoid looking at her; their gazes collided in a clumsy mess of blues. She was wearing false lashes, he noted, and her lips had been overlined with purple, completely disregarding the traditional theme of the ball.

Lottie would *hate* her.

The song picked up at that point, and they spun faster, twisting and turning, the elf looping under his arm. All of the elves in the Noël Region knew how to dance like this, to carols and violins, trained as children to be prepared for such events. She was good, all feet and hands and hips making the right moves in time to the music, clearly well-practised, maybe an elf of high status. She laughed off Abe's jilted actions, the awkwardness as his elbow collided with her shoulder, as if she were used to bad dancing and perhaps even found it endearing.

"I'm Mollie, by the way!" she called, over the sound of the

instruments. "You're Abraham Cane, aren't you? My dad sends all our shoes to your shop every year. We get new ones imported from America each Christmastime."

Abe wanted to point out that if they just kept their old shoes and bought new ones for the disadvantaged kids then it would save all the bother, but he couldn't quite bring himself to. Instead, he smiled and nodded as Mollie continued to talk, mouth opening and closing at a rapid speed.

"It's a lovely shop. My dad's always saying how nice it is... and great for the world, as well!"

Abe nodded, forcing another smile, one which tickled his jaw.

"My parents own a luxury restaurant, see. It's very bespoke, quite exclusive, so you mightn't have been... the Gingerbread Restaurant, just off Tinsel Street?"

She was watching him now, carefully, with nose blue eyes like slits. She knew he'd been there with Patrick that night. This was no coincidence. She wanted to know his status, why he'd visited with a boy that day. If he were outed by this blonde elf, right in the middle of Santa's Christmas Ball, it'd ruin his parents' reputation completely... not to mention his own.

Trying to keep an impassive expression on his face, he cocked his head to one side and said, "Yes, I do know it. I went with a good friend of mine a few weeks back. It's a wonderful restaurant, Mollie!"

With that, her eyes opened up and she grinned. That was all she wanted, evidently. Now with a toothy smile alight across her face, she pulled back as they twisted into a spin, her shrieking with laughter and diving under his arm, as the music played on into the night.

They danced for a good half hour or so, until they were

out of breath and sweating, pink in the face and filled to the brim with laughter. Abe held out a hand to tug her over to the drinks table, and they went with the casual ease of a couple, comfortable in each other's space and clinging to arms and elbows.

"What would you like?" he asked, scouring the table. He turned his head a little, catching Mollie's eye.

She was staring back at him with the look of a tiger, surveying its prey. "I'd like..." she began, nibbling her bottom lip. Abe watched, face flushed, as her eyes wandered over the selection. "Apple gin and tonic water, please."

He made their drinks in two fancy cocktail glasses, meeting her at the nearby table, where she perched. The ballroom was alive again, the dancefloor full and the tables mostly bare, adults standing with their glasses as they mingled and picked at the remaining hors-d'œuvres. They drank in silence for a moment, watching the dancing, before Abe felt something slide across his thigh under the table and instantly froze.

Mollie's expression was perfectly demure and innocent as she continued to look forward, eyes trained on the dancers. Her hand, however, slipped further over his leg and between both, one finger rubbing gently at the inside of his thigh, making tiny circling motions. Abe's heart was in his mouth as she slid further up, right at the edge of his zip, eyes searching for permission.

"Outside," she mouthed, rising from her chair and reaching out to grab his hand. Silently, he took it.

They left the ballroom through the main hall, which was now empty. Instead of going through the main doors and out into the gardens, however, Mollie pulled him the opposite way, up the winding staircase that led to the bathrooms and the first floor, which held guest suites and the library.

"This way," she murmured, footsteps light on the carpet. "It'll be empty. It always is…"

Allowing her to lead him, they hurried down a passage and to a large door, which was latched shut. Fiddling with the door for a second, it fell open before them as Mollie dragged him into the room.

It *was* the library she'd taken him to, a dark room with ceiling-high shelving units and leather furniture, two armchairs overlooking the grounds through a wide, latticed window. The carpet was dark green and the walls were papered thickly in browns and reds, and the books were each faded and yellowing, the spins cracked and dusty.

"It's like stepping back in time," she said, smiling and breathing in deeply. "Don't you agree, Abraham?"

Without saying a word, he nodded.

She was right, in a way. It was like reaching into a time before them, and he was grateful for the way it pulled him for reality, even if just for a second.

With a seductive curl of her finger, Mollie beckoned him over to one of the leather armchairs. Abe fell back into it and sunk into its musty scent as she dropped on top of him, skirts riding up around her legs and eyes glowing icy blue in the dim lamplight. He nodded, hoping she'd take the lead, all of the hurt coming back to him in a sudden wave… and Mollie wasn't going to think twice.

She unzipped him in a matter of seconds, twisting round for him to undo the button at the top of her backless dress, before slipping out of it and throwing it onto the floor beside her. Heart thumping wildly and eyes unsure of where to look next, he clutched her back nervously, just to look like he was doing something. It didn't feel right. None of this did. And yet something inside was spurring him on, something impossible to out into words. A feeling not quite tangible, real.

There wasn't much else going through Abe's mind, at that point.

Just anger.

Blazing, white-flushed anger.

But who exactly was it directed at?

"We only have a few minutes," she whispered, breath hot against his ear. "Someone will notice we're missing." Pressing up against him, she murmured, "It's cute how nervous you are, Abraham. This... this isn't your *first time*, is it?"

Abe shook his head. It wasn't a lie, exactly... but this was his first time with a girl, and he had no idea how to handle it.

Just think about Patrick, think about Patrick, think about Patrick...

Patrick, his bare, golden skin, soft, floppy stomach...

This girl *wanted* him.

But he didn't want her, did he? Not right now, like this.

As angry as he was at Patrick, he couldn't do this. It didn't make sense to him. It wasn't *right*.

"I'm sorry," he said, shaking his head. "I can't. Not like this. You deserve... better. You deserve for it to be special."

And although Mollie looked momentarily disappointed, then relieved, it seemed to satisfy her.

What was he *doing*? How could he *do* that to someone? He watched as she began to pull her dress back on, then reached to button it for her. She was nodding at him, like she'd made up her mind, expression unreadable.

They walked back down to the ballroom with hands held, Abe rapidly trying to quell his doubts. It was good, wasn't it, what he'd told her, his promises? Mollie seemed nice, and liked him, and he… liked her. He'd be fine – he'd give his parents exactly what they wanted. And Mollie…

Well, she was certainly very pretty, that he could tell. Maybe they could be happy together?

He squeezed her hand, more to reassure himself, as they wandered back through the door and into the ball. Santa's eldest son, Nick, late forties and hairy, hairy all over, was stood near them with a group of factory owners. He was nodding and picking at his beard to make sure there weren't bits of hors-d'œuvres still stuck to it, greedy eyes navigating the ball.

Mr and Mrs Cane were a little way off, and looked up in surprise as Abe entered with Mollie, clocking the joint hands instantly. The look on his mother's face was priceless, and she turned to her husband eagerly.

Abe led Mollie over to them, letting go of her hand and grinning.

"Mum? Dad? This is Mollie. Her parents own the Gingerbread Restaurant."

"Ah, you're Cyril's daughter!" Mr Cane shook her hand, nodding his respect. "Great family, great family! And how do you know Abraham?"

"Oh, we're very good friends." She smirked at him, adjusting her dress slightly. "Your son's an excellent young man, Mr Cane. You should be very proud."

"Oh, we are," Mrs Cane replied, shaking her head and allowing herself to tear up a little. "So, so proud –"

"Abe!"

At first, Abe thought he was imagining it.

The voice.

A voice.

A voice, in his ear, calling his name from across the room.

His parents and Mollie hadn't noticed. They proceeded to talk about their businesses and Mollie's father amiably, laughing, smiling, feverish, nodding.

Abe, however, couldn't settle. He glanced around the room, heart pounding.

He'd know that voice anywhere.

"Abe!"

There it was again. Closer this time; a shout.

Mollie spun around to him, frowning, and followed his gaze across the ballroom.

There was no denying it; not now. For there, a little way off through the hordes of dancers, was Patrick.

He was dressed in what Abe assumed to be his best clothes, belly held tight inside a too-small suit jacket and skinny chinos. He'd pushed his hair back with far too much gel and was smiling anxiously, brown eyes like melted chocolate, squashed against Abe's in the heat of the room.

"Lottie said I'd find you here," he started, expression hopeful. "I was worried I wouldn't get up the drive because of that old myth – you know, the one about the grounds only letting in people who truly *need* to come here – but I guess Santa knew how much I needed this. Abe, I'm so sorry for what happened, I –"

At that moment, Nick came strolling out from the gathering crowd behind them. His beard was all mussed up and he looked baffled, holding something in one hand; a scroll. The band had stopped playing and spectators were staring between them, confused, as Abe wished for the floor to swallow him whole.

"Who are *you*?" Nick asked, staring at Patrick and looking at the list of parchment in his hand. "You weren't invited, were you?"

"No, Sir," Patrick responded quickly. "I'm here to tell Abraham Cane that I love him."

And with that, he turned back to Abe, shaking his head and gazing at him with such intensity that Abe felt his stomach swill inside him.

This couldn't be happening.

"Because I do love you, Abe. I'm so sorry for everything I said. I don't care about our situations, or if we'll one day live to regret this… I love you, and that's all that matters. I want to be with you. I *need* to be with you. I –"

"What *is* this nonsense?" Nick burst, staring between them with pink cheeks. "Abraham, do you love this… this… *boy*?"

Abe was bright red now, face practically aglow, body on fire. Mollie was watching him, eyes narrowed, and his parents shaking their heads, the picture of disappointment.

He couldn't look at Patrick again.

If he did, the look on his face would make his answer clear.

"I… no," he eventually said, shortly, voice sore, hoarse. "No, I don't love Patrick, Sir. He's just a friend of mine who must have had a little too much to drink –"

"Thank goodness," Nick said, letting out a short sigh of relief. "This is absolutely preposterous. You, boy, get out now, before I have you arrested! How dare you come in here, shouting your false accusations and making a fool out of yourself like that! This is broadcast to the entirety of the North Pole, I'll have you know. Do you really think you'll ever find work now that you've been *exposed*?"

Abe couldn't avoid glancing at Patrick for any longer, for his heart was breaking in two and he *needed* to see him, to show with his expression that he was sorry, somehow.

But Patrick's bottom lip was quivering and he was shaking

his head in pure fury, eyes glossed over with unshed tears.

"After everything we've been through... I really thought you'd do the right thing." And that was it. Patrick stormed past him, shaking with anger.

Gasps rippled across the room, followed by a sharp intake of breath from Nick, who was turning redder and redder by the second.

And Mollie. Mollie, who was egging him on, who'd already decided he was her perfect husband candidate and wouldn't stop at anything to make him hers, even if he'd never love her... not like *that*.

Patrick stopped at the door, staring Abe straight in the eye.

For a moment, everyone else in the room simply disappeared; it was Patrick and Abe, always, just the two of them, like it was meant to be.

"I hope you're happy now, Abe. I really, really do."

Dear Abe,

I write this sitting on a bench, biting my thumbnail, wishing I could somehow go back in time and twist the North Pole on its axis, making everything right again.

But I can't. This is the last time I'm going to write to you, sent or unsent. And with this letter, I'm going to attempt to move on.

I don't think about the past much - I don't think it's worth dwelling on things long gone - but I too once thought that I'd never find love. When I first starting dating Dora, we were young and naïve, and I didn't yet know I liked guys too. I thought there was something wrong with me when I couldn't make it work. She was confused too... confused about why we, no matter how hard we tried, found it awkward to kiss, and to hug, and to spend time together with this huge, romantic expectation over our shoulders.

Then I realised we simply weren't right for each other, that we were better off as friends, and I started to wonder whether maybe I'd ever really be right for anyone.

But you, Abe... you taught me how to love. You taught me how to be vulnerable, open, how to grasp onto life with both hands and scream into the wind, because that's what life is for; the living, the loving, the experiences along the way. You may not see yourself as the most positive of people (your gentle cynicism is much admired), but I see an appreciation inside of you, an appreciation for everything you do. You see wonder where most see darkness, even if you don't always notice.

I really wanted things to work out between us, but what I see now is that you and me... we were an experience, a pure love which existed for a moment, a week, maybe two, and made its mark. It made its mark on me, on my heart, taught me so much about myself. You, Abe, somehow made me more... me.

I wish you all the best in your life, I really do. It's not easy. No path is. You might have all the privileges I once thought you should enjoy, but I have a family who love and accept me, and I see now that maybe riches aren't black and white. My riches come in the form of people; that's something money can't buy.

Lots of love and sprinkles, always,
        Patrick xxx

PART TWO

the north pole
december 2013

SIXTEEN

Somewhere, in a hospital in the North Pole, a man sat at a bench, staring out of the window. Snow covered a stretch of tarmac holding hansom cabs and bicycles, filling the empty space and sheltering patches from the storm. A couple wandered past with arms linked; they didn't bother looking through the glass at the old, sad man. The man whose blue eyes were watering and whose nose ran unstopped, whose shoelaces had been left untied for so long he couldn't remember how they were once done up.

Sat in a hospital corridor, the remnants of hair on his head snow white and underarms reeking of candy cane eau de toilette, he watched the world go by. In the thin, papery gown they'd dressed him in, he could just see the outline of his knobbly knees and sagging thighs. Ribs stuck out from a layer of wizened plastic, freckles turned dark with age.

He stretched, the skin of his wrists dripping off of him, hairs sparse. Nowhere on his body contained substantial flesh, but his limbs were the most spindly, especially as he tried to stand. He pushed up from the bench and, now on his feet, reached for the walking stick beside him.

It was going to be a long, long journey.

His doctor's room was on the top floor; he was on the

bottom. It took a good five minutes to reach the end of the corridor, which was thin and green, not the festive kind, and seemed to drag on and on and on. At the entrance to the staircase, he straightened up and tapped the floor several times with his stick, testing it out. Each step felt like it lasted an age, his lungs screaming for air as he dragged himself to the next floor, and the next, and the next. Toes numb in their rubber sliders, he stopped to rub them, leaning back against the wall to catch his breath.

Only a few more steps…

The door read "Dr. Montana", and was situated to the left of him. It was firmly shut. After three raps of his knuckles, a call came from within. The old man pushed down on the handle, then peeled his way into the room, gasping for breath.

"Abraham Cane!" Dr. Montana greeted him, rushing to pull out his chair. He was a tall elf, with dark skin and a head of thick hair, and had the richest of smiles, wasted on the old man. "How wonderful it is to see you again! How have you been keeping these last few days?"

But Abe wasn't stupid. He could detect the sympathy in Dr Montana's voice, that horrid, stilted awkwardness, and frowned.

"I've been keeping well," he said, in a tone more than a tad sarcastic. "I can't eat, I can't sleep, I can't even pee without excruciating pain… I must say, Doctor, that I'm feeling pretty *fabulous*."

Dr. Montana frowned, glancing down at the piece of paper before him. "Yes… it says here that your wife died several years back, in a sledging accident? It must be very hard, Mr Cane, going home each day to an empty house and having to cope with your pain alone. Do you make all of your own meals, shop for yourself, that sort of thing?"

Abe rolled his eyes and jiggled his knee in discomfort, a nervous tick he still couldn't remove, thirty years later. "Mollie's absence does make things harder, I suppose. But I manage. I'm not like these youths of today, who think they can get out of anything with a good enough excuse and a touch of cold."

"Do you have any children, Mr Cane? It says here that there were... *complications*."

"Mollie and I couldn't have children." His teeth were gritted as he spat this, staring down at the table. Even now, the irony of it all still rankled.

He'd gotten used to his marriage, to Mollie, to the running of his father's business... but the fact that they'd never been blessed with babies was something he couldn't get over.

As if giving up Patrick had been tough enough for twenty-year-old, naïve Abe, growing up to disappoint his parents all over again had been even worse. Nobody to carry on the firm, to take over the shoe business... that was all they saw. In the end, it hadn't mattered if Abe married a man or a woman; his parents despised him all the same.

"So, you have no one at home to help you out?" the doctor checked. "I really don't think that's sensible, Mr Cane. You're getting weaker. There are several homes for... *the unwell*, especially here in Noël. They cook all your meals for you, do your shopping, your washing, clean your room... I've heard good things from previous patients who've moved into residential homes, and been extremely well looked after, I must say." He paused, sensing uncertainty. "How do you like the sound of that, Mr Cane? It says here that you were a business owner, back in the day. I assume you're not strapped for cash."

"Am I, heck!"

After selling the shoe shop a few months back to fund his retirement, he wasn't wasting a single penny of it on some tacky retirement home. Especially not now that he was living in his parents' house, the house he'd grown up in, all by himself, with Lottie and her family just opposite.

He tried to imagine going back to sharing facilities with someone, having to cope with the stress and drama of cohabitation, but the idea made him nauseous.

"I have friends, Dr. Montana – ever heard of that concept? They'll help me out, if it gets to that point. Not that it will, of course."

Clearing his throat, the doctor shuffled his papers again and glanced down at his desk.

"See... the thing is, Mr Cane, it *will* come to that. We've had your test results back, and they're not good, I'm afraid." Dr. Montana licked his fingers in order to turn the page, and pulled out another sheaf of papers from a drawer under the table. They were covered in green and red writing, boxes and stats and grids laid out across them. "Your blood tests were alarming, and so the scan we took – the full body one, from two weeks ago – showed several dark areas within your bowel and pelvic region, spreading upwards."

The room was silent.

Dark areas? Abe had read enough reports in the local newspaper to know what *that* meant, but he still couldn't seem to process it... or more so didn't *want* to figure out the implications of those words.

He watched the doctor's expression carefully, not daring to glance away.

"You got my results back?" he repeated. "And? Tell me

what they said, you stupid elf!"

Slowly, Dr. Montana pushed a sheet of paper towards Abe. Everything seemed to happen in slow motion. Abe dared not look down at the desk, vision blurring as he skimmed the numbers, the boxes, the little graphs and figures.

"You have three months left to live, Mr Cane. You're in the final stages of a severe elfness which has entered several of your organs, as shown on the diagram below, and is infiltrating your entire body. I'm sorry we weren't able to pick this up earlier." He paused, genuinely looking sorry for Abe, kind face wary. "Please, take all the time you need to process this."

An *elfness*.

No – it couldn't be. He wasn't that old. Most elves lived long, happy lives. He was lying; he *had* to be lying.

Abe shook his head at the doctor. He pulled out his fist and smashed it against the table weakly, eyes filling with dry tears.

"No!" he whispered, voice hoarse. "You must be mistaken. I can't have *three months* left."

"I'm so sorry," the doctor repeated. "Would you like me to get someone to pick you up, Mr Cane? The friends you were talking about, perhaps?"

Abe just shook his head, frail body shaking, partly with shock and yet somehow almost with… *fury*. "No, no, they needn't bother coming out. I think I just need to sit here a while, process it. Any chance of a coffee?"

But the doctor shook his head, eyeing the door guiltily. "Actually… I can't let you stay in here, as I'm due to see another patient in five minutes or so. I'm sorry, Mr Cane. There's the snowflake room down the corridor, where our patients usually go to grieve or deal with hard news. There are beanbags, magazines, a coffee machine in there... I can show you there now, if you'd like?"

Abe stared at him incredulously, scarcely able to believe what he was hearing. "The sodding *snowflake room*? Don't patronise me!"

"I just thought –"

"You're all the same, you doctors! You ruin us with a sentence, and you think you're the saviours of the earth!" Still gasping for breath, Abe pushed back and reached for his walking stick, standing up beside Dr. Montana. "And I'll be seeing you next Christmas, blooming know-all. Three months, my arse!"

If we're to tell this story, you must see the whole picture. How did we get here, to Abe's fifties, of all places, you might ask? That's a question I don't have a straight-forward answer to, I'm afraid.

Earlier the previous morning, Abraham Cane awoke in his bed, the bed which had held his parents before him, and his grandparents before that, and stretched.

Today was the day.

He'd received a letter from Doctor Montana, who gave him a scan and a striped candy cane sometime in November, inviting him to go back into hospital and receive the results.

This was exactly the sort of thing he needed Mollie for.

It had been almost thirty years since he met her at Santa's Ball, saw her gliding towards him in a cloud of pretty fabric and blonde hair.

Thirty years.

A lot could happen in thirty years.

You could fall in love, have children, travel. You could take up a new hobby, perhaps cookery or dance, or start a micro-herb garden in your greenhouse.

Abe had done none of those things.

What was the point? That was his motto, as his years ran away and he sat on the same old recliner, feet up, a big bowl of sour cream snowballs to his side.

What was the flipping point?

But suddenly you're fifty, and you're old, and you have an incurable elfness, like so many elves develop, only earlier, too soon, unexpected.

You're sat on the same recliner, hand in a bowl of snowballs, wondering when you let it all go to waste.

The point becomes clear.

This isn't an unhappy tale, though. Abe got up, washed his body in the shower, combed his sparse hair and pulled on clothes, a cap. He packed a hospital bag as they'd told him he could be stayi-

-ng overnight, and wondered whether, somewhere in the world, some poor elf was doing the same, packing their bags for hospital, crying because life would never be the same again.

And Abe felt, for the first time in years, compassion.

It was such a start feeling, he'd almost forgotten what it felt like.

He hailed a cab, tipping the driver, and walked the last few metres to the hospital, before collapsing on a bench, chest burning and eyes blazing red.

That was when it hit him.

The anger. Abe wasn't stupid. He knew, in his heart of hearts, that he didn't have long left. How could he, when he could barely make it to the hospital without crashing?

And he could only blame himself.

He'd wasted it, these last thirty years. In fact, he'd wasted his whole entire life. It wasn't just Patrick, but all of it. His hopes, his dreams, any chance of friends or fun. What had he been living for?

This isn't meant to be a sad ending, it really isn't.

But if you take anything from Abe's story… let it be that you only have one life, one chance at happiness.

Live it.

SEVENTEEN

The cab took far too long to arrive as Abe stood, freezing, on the side of the road. He'd thrown a coat on over his thin hospital gown, and was staring into the distance as snow fell around him, landing on his pale eyelashes and leaving a ghostly outline to his shadow.

The hospital was an imposing building, made from red brick and thick black windows, masking the white and green corridors beyond. The sign on the door was flashing with red fairy lights, hardly the most inviting welcome. Abe frowned, tapping his walking stick on the side of his leg to wake it up.

He *hated* the cold. Always had done.

It was winter in the North Pole, a season for love and for giving, their favourite time of the year. Summer here rarely got the hazy heights of Barbados or Miami, but winter was positively nose-numbing, temperatures dipping well below minus ten. You'd think Abe would be used to it by now... but somehow, he'd gotten more and more grouchy across the years. He was an enemy of snow, hated the frost and fog, and was a firm believer in sunshine and cloudless skies.

The hansom cab pulled up a few moments later, driven by a cocky young elf with roasted red cheeks and a huge grin that stretched the length of his face.

He doffed his cap as Abe hoisted himself up, asking, "Where to?" in a false Cockney accent – no doubt adopted from watching *Only Fools and Horses* box sets on his imported television.

"Back Lane, Noël Region," Abe said gruffly, huffing and puffing as he shuffled into a comfy position. The wind blew up his thin gown and froze his nether regions half solid, so he pulled his coat tight around himself, for fear of catching hypothermia – or worse.

"Just been to an appointment, 'ave ye'?" the driver called back to him, the grin of someone trying to seem friendly dancing across his face. "Bad news, was it? Ye' seem a bit down in the dumps!"

Abe frowned, turning his head so that he didn't have to see the sparkling blue eyes or cheerful white teeth, which, combined, were enough to make him nauseous.

The cab pulled up outside his house in the nick of time, pulling to a stop as the driver reached out to take his coins. Abe dropped a few into his palm and snorted rudely, flicking away his fingers as he climbed down the steps.

There'd be no tips for *him*, the conceited beggar.

Careful on the ice, Abe made his way to the front door. It had been peeling for a while now and the letter box always jammed up when it was cold, but he pushed through anyway, relief flooding through him. The central heating he'd had installed was working perfectly, and he dropped his keys and walking stick onto the table by the front door with a blunt sigh.

How *wonderful* it was to be home.

He poured himself a bowl of sour cream snowballs and a glass of Pepsi from the fridge, growling as he tried to open the can. Sticky brown liquid fizzed up over the edges, all over the kitchen side. One remote control and three channel changes later, he was sat in front of the television he too had imported from the continent, an anniversary present for Mollie several years back, legs wide open. His hospital gown was hanging off him in a soggy mess, but the fire crackled before him, melting his icy joints.

Blooming doctors, thinking they knew it all...

It was at that moment that a rocket of pain shot across his body, from his bowels to his shoulders, causing him to wince and double over. It was like tiny sparks were pushing through his skin, desperate to leave, burning through flesh and sparse muscle. Bile swelled over his tongue and through his teeth as he coughed into a tissue, shoulders locked into place and eyes streaming.

"Bauble-bearing... blooming... elfness!" he wheezed. "Three months... my... backside!"

A horrendous cough hacked through him, painful against the back of his throat. Eyes watering, he straightened up and leaned back against the chair, hands shaking against his knees.

The television was still playing, a re-run of the British TV show *Bargain Hunt*. He could barely see the screen. His eyes were so watery, so full of dry tears and thick gunge, that keeping them open was a strain.

You're in the final stages of a severe elfness which has entered several of your organs, as shown on the diagram below, and is infiltrating your entire body... Abe swallowed, shaking his head back and forth, back and forth. He could feel it, though; that was undeniable. The elfness, spreading through his organs, his lungs, like a huge, black cloud.

He barely even heard the knock on the door. As it sounded again, he wearily rapped three times on the coffee table, a gesture for them to enter – or a cry for help.

The sound of footsteps was heard in the corridor, and Abe glanced up. Two children ran into the room, messy curls spread across their foreheads, brown eyes wide and solemn. With sticky mouths and eager expressions, they cried, "Uncle Abe, Uncle Abe!" and proceeded to pat along his bald head and arms.

"Okay, okay!" he said gruffly, pulling away in alarm. "Uncle Abe's not feeling too good, kids. How about you go play in the garden for a bit, leave me to talk to your mum and dad?" He watched as the youngest propelled itself across the room, placing a moist hand flat against the face of the presenter. "Edward, get away from my TV set! There'll be no Christmas presents for you if you ruin the screen!"

"You only ever buy us snowballs anyway, Uncle Abe," Sarah said demurely, sticking out a pink tongue at him. "And we don't even *like* the sweet chilli ones – only sour cream!"

"Yes, well, well." Abe rolled his eyes, gesturing for her to leave. "I eat the sour cream snowballs myself, Sarah. It's called *conserving your goods*."

"And giving us the bads!" she retorted, spinning round and flushing as her parents entered the room, stripped of their winter clothes and wearing sensible jeans and jumpers, socks fuzzy against the plush carpet. "Mum, Dad! Uncle Abe isn't feeling well!"

Her mother turned to Abe with a frown, reaching out to check his temperature.

Even years later, Lottie couldn't help but act like a mother figure to him. It didn't matter where they were, or what they were doing…

She'd always be his soulmate.

After Mollie died, Lottie had washed his clothes and

hoovered the house for months, still nipping round with her duster every now and then, bottle of fabric spray in hand. She felt his head and cheeks now, eyes narrowed, then pulled back with a frown.

"Kids, can you go outside, please?" She glanced up to fix Edward and Sarah with a glare. "Now. The snow is still fresh; you can build a snowman!"

Standing up begrudgingly, they moved outside, soon snorting with laughter as their feet hit the snow and a snowball fight commenced. Abe watched them through the window, the snowballs on his lap suddenly a whole lot less appealing.

Three months.

Three months.

Simon – Lottie's long-standing, patient, rather wet husband – perched opposite Abe, on the pouffe, trying for a smile. Lottie sat next to him, stomach dipping over the top of her jeans.

"Abe?" she said, though her voice quivered and he knew from her face what she was going to say next. "You got your test results back, didn't you?"

Abe was silent as he nodded, the light shining off his bald head. Tears immediately sprung to Lottie's eyes, as she shook her head and reached to grasp Simon.

Fingers trembling, she added, "And?"

"It's an elfness." His voice was flat as he stared back, gaze steady. "The stupid arse told me I have three months to live, but I told him where to shove *that* information."

The minute the words left his mouth, he could see Lottie's whole demeanour crumble, and his stomach dropped. Simon scooped her up with a weak arm. Her face was all scrunched up, the noise escaping her mouth sounding almost... animal, like that of a polar bear struck by poachers. He watched helplessly as she bawled against his front room.

There was nothing else to say as she continued to cry, cradled by Simon and yet somehow loose, disjointed, like she wasn't part of reality. It didn't *feel* like reality, either. Part of Abe wanted to burst into tears with her and another part – the stronger side of him, the delusional, holding-onto-hope part – refused to believe it was even happening.

It was a nightmare, that's what it was.

"How… how're you taking it?" Simon flushed pink at his horrifically awkward phrasing. "I just mean… are you coping with the news well, or…"

"I'm dealing *fabulously*, Simon," Abe replied drolly. He glanced at his best friend again, swallowing hard at her swollen face and puffy eyes. "Lottie, love, please don't cry. You're not helping."

"I'm sorry," she muttered, wiping her eyes on the back of her hands. "It's just… *Abe*, three months isn't long, not at all. There's still so much we want to do, want to see, together…"

"And we will! The three months they've given me is a load of diarrhoea, Lotts. I have years and years left in me."

But as Lottie glanced at him – eyes roaming over his tired eyes, sagging skin, the off-colour freckles and his pale, bald head – the look that passed between them suggested they both knew he didn't have his estimated "years".

"We just want what's best for you," she murmured, trying for a smile. "We'll do whatever you want to make you happy, Abe, over the next few weeks. Anything you particularly want to do… we're your people."

Abe rolled his eyes. "I'd quite like to watch the rest of this show in peace, if I'm honest. These snowballs won't eat themselves."

Simon and Lottie glanced at each other, blushing, and began to get up from the pouffe. "Yes, of course. Sorry, we just…"

Simon rushed to the door to pull the kids inside, almost slipping over in his Santa socks, while Lottie stood near Abe and watched him. He was staring at the TV, eyes narrowed and hand dipped into the bowl of snowballs, but the slight tremor of his lip and the moistness of his blue eyes told her that maybe, just maybe, he wasn't feeling quite as brave as he made out.

"We're here for you," she said, voice trembling. Her hand slipped over the arm of the chair to switch off the television, and he flinched. "There'll come a time when you need us, Abe – when you want to let us in. And when that time comes, we'll be there."

Slowly, he nodded. It was only a slight tap of the chin, hardly distinguishable, but Lottie smiled and linked fingers with him despite it. "We're just across the road. Knock if you need anything, okay?"

Simon came back into the room at that moment, Sarah and Edward in front, grinning and soaking wet. Sarah had a snowball locked in one hand, just hidden beneath her coat, and Abe winked as he noticed her lift it.

"Got you!" she cried, expression ecstatic as snow dripped down her mother's face, quenching the top of her jumper. "You didn't see that coming, Mum!"

"And you didn't see *this* coming," Lottie retorted, pointing a furious finger towards the door. "No TV for two nights, missus. And no crisps, either!"

"Aw, Mum!" Sarah objected, face falling. "It was only a *joke*…"

"Outside, now!" Lottie instructed. "You too, Edward." She

turned to Abe, squeezing tight. "Remember what I said, okay? And you're welcome for tea at our house any time. We're making fajitas tonight, Simon's speciality."

"Thanks," Abe replied gruffly. "I might take you up on that offer."

"We love you, Abe. Don't forget that, okay? We're right here."

"I know," he said, unable to look her in the eye for fear that she'd notice the gathering tears. "I know."

The door closed softly behind them.

Almost thirty years ago, now, Abe and Lottie's new lives had begun. Snow was falling all around the North Pole, and somewhere, far into the distance, Abe swore he could hear carol singers warbling. But maybe that was just his imagination. He closed his eyes and breathed in deeply, opening them again as the organ began to play, and the whole church stood to watch.

Down the aisle floated Lottie, on a cloud of white lace, the biggest of smiles on her pretty face. She waved left and right to her family and Simon's, stopping when she reached Abe, somewhere by the altar.

And then she was climbing, high into the sky, up the steps towards Simon. He was smiling at her like she was the most beautiful elf in all the land… and in that moment, she probably was. Her hair was curly and fell in ringlets around her face, and her lips were pursed and painted plum.

All eyes were on her.

Lottie had gotten her happy ending, Abe thought, as the proceedings began. A husband, marriage, true love… Simon was in it for the long run.

He turned to his side, where Mollie was stood, hands clasped in front of her, eyes fixed on the front of the room. She was wearing red and green eyeshadow in pastel shades, very on-theme, and a candy cane dress to match the huge engagement ring on her hand. It had cost Abe an arm and a leg, picked out by his mother, of course, who insisted it would follow in Cane family tradition.

His eyes cut back to the front of the room, to his best friend, a beaming ray of sunshine, under the dappled light of the church's stained glass. The windows were each decorated with Santa Claus figures symbolising the ten regions of the North Pole, but the Noël figure was in the centre, smiling proudly, like he could imagine Nick was right now, wherever he was.

Abe's blood still boiled when he thought back to that night at Santa's Ball, but there was nothing he could do about it now.

The wedding continued in a kaleidoscope of pastel confetti and little Christmas-coloured macaroons, Lottie, the centre of attention at last, her company's pastries decorating table upon table, covering a whole cake stand with cupcakes and chocolate-dipped strawberries.

Abe reached for a mince pie cocktail, but it wasn't as good as the one from the Gingerbread Restaurant. They'd supped a whole bucketload on the night of the engagement, before Mollie dragged him home to talk business in front of the fire, admiring her ring with greedy blue eyes.

She was there now, clinging onto his arm, smiling, laughing with his parents, who were there to celebrate Lottie's big day too.

Abe's tie was too tight, trousers suffocating him.

He felt like he was drowning - or being drowned.

Like someone was holding a great vat of cinnamon vodka over his face, making him gasp for air.

He wanted to be happy for his friend, he really did. But when he looked at Lottie, all Abe saw was a list of things he could never have, a list of things he so desperately wanted but couldn't grab with one hand, let alone two.

Happiness, the kind you're supposed to feel at Christmas.

And true love.

Only Abe had experienced true love, once. A year ago, months before his engagement to Mollie.

And he'd thrown it all away for this.

EIGHTEEN

For a while, Abe simply sat and stared at the fireplace before him. His throat still ached and his body was tense, and the room around him felt cold, desolate. Even the sofa was hard beneath him, like he'd only just realised it was made from rock.

Across from him, a photo sat in a frame. It was one he hadn't had the heart to remove after Mollie died, despite pushing every other copy of her face into the cupboard under the stairs. It was a nice one. The only nice one.

He frowned at the mantlepiece, at that perfect photograph in its perfect silver frame, full of smiling faces and neat hair, an onslaught of white.

Grasping his stick, he stood to inspect it properly.

It'd been taken on their wedding day, a July date, amidst the North Pole's artificial summer. Seven months or so after he stood in the crowd at Lottie's. He was standing beside Mollie with her arm clasped firmly around him, a smile fixed onto his face.

She looked beautiful, of course, all dressed in white with a demure blonde bun placed high on her neck, neckline plunging right down to her belly. She only ever wore backless dresses, he soon found out, in the months after Santa's

Christmas Ball. If the dress wasn't backless, it was an *especially* special occasion.

Beneath that dress, there'd been nude underwear to rival that of the night of the ball, bits of lace and string fashioned into a pair of tiny knickers. They fell asleep straight after the wedding; the couple knew what they were doing, didn't even bother to share a kiss. The love between them was performative, and they both knew it. It was there – strong and endearing, loyal – but never romantic.

But, three years after his wife died, the love he'd once forced started to… dissolve. It settled in the form of fondness, more than anything. There's only so long you can keep up the pretence when it's gnawing at your soul, desperate to get out, *let loose*. He didn't like women. He'd never loved Mollie the way she wanted him to, even if he'd had love – vague, non-specific love – for her, once.

It was men he wanted – and, more specifically, Patrick.

And so he couldn't keep her pictures up, couldn't even think about his wife, consumed by an overwhelming sense of guilt, one he never thought he'd feel when she was alive.

Now that she was gone, however, there was nothing else to occupy his mind. He was a single man; he could do what he wanted, anything, even. He thought about men every waking second, his whole body tingling with envy as he watched them on TV, in the train station, on the street, in parks… everywhere, and yet so far from him.

"It was *obvious* that this would happen," Lottie had told him, time and time again. "You never loved Mollie, everyone could see that. I don't think she even loved you. You were convenient for each other. That's all."

"Thanks, Lotts," he'd reply, expression flat. "That makes me feel *so* much better."

He tried everything to make the feelings go away, to make himself want her. But like Lottie said, it wasn't as if Mollie had ever truly wanted him too. She wanted a husband, the title, stability. It was convenient for them both, especially once they found out they couldn't have children, started sleeping in separate beds.

And now, sat in his living room in a papery hospital gown, voice hoarse and body stinging with pain, wracked through and through with evil cells, he couldn't help but think… for what? For what had he lived a life of misery, slept alone in a cold double bed, sat in silence over glasses of wine his wife poured, wine he never wanted? For what had he married Mollie, attempted to have her children, a family, if it was never going to make him happy?

The happiest he'd ever been in his life was with Patrick, that weekend. Nothing since had even come *close* to topping it.

Yet he couldn't think about Patrick without burning with fury and regret, body cringing at his actions.

Had twenty-year-old Abe really been so *stupid*?

Evidently so.

Now, he whacked his walking stick against the fireplace in anger and glared at the figure staring back in the mirror. Bald, pale, stick-thin and shivering; he didn't even recognise himself anymore.

"Blooming elfness!" he cried suddenly, tears filling his eyes properly and blurring his vision. "Why can't you just sod off and leave me alone!"

But there was no answer.

He left for Lottie and Simon's at four, hobbling across the road through the snow with his stick as a guide. The house opposite was significantly similar in size and stature, yet

Simon was forever repainting the doors and window frames, and the tubs of plants outside and on the lawn were always green and cheerful, kept alive throughout winter with a touch of North Pole magic. He knocked, leaning against the wood so as to catch his breath, and almost fell forwards as it opened beneath him.

"Abe!" Simon exclaimed, smiling widely. "Come in, come in! You couldn't resist my fajitas after all, I see…"

The house inside was small and curvy and beige, full of furniture and circles, handmade decorations and pictures hanging from every surface. Sarah had been crafting stockings for a school project, and they drooped from the banister in a long, sagging line, all misplaced stitches and sad buttons. Edward always left toy cars scattered along the floorboards, and Abe had to step carefully so he wouldn't crush them, rolling his eyes as Simon led him up the hall and into the warm space.

The kitchen smelt strongly of cumin, an aroma which wafted from a pan of frying onions. Tortillas lay on plates around the room, stacks of three different varieties, beside pots of salsa, guac and sour cream, and a bowl of mince sat beside the stove, ready to fry off, two ripe avocados perched on the shelf above.

"It smells wonderful," Abe said, awkwardly. He'd never really got on with Simon, even after thirty years of living close by, sharing weekly catchups over a meal. Their conversation was stilted, too much blushing and repeating of sentences, stumbling over words and mixing up phrases. Simon was wet, bland, dull, balancing Lottie's crazy.

But all Abe had ever wanted was for someone to love his best friend completely and utterly for who she was and that was exactly what Simon did.

"Abe!" came a voice from behind him, as Lottie burst into the room. She grinned and rushed to hug him, throwing her arms around him and squeezing, tight. "Take a seat!"

Tea was served just minutes later, at the dining room table. They ate ridiculous amounts, as was the unbreakable rule at Lottie's house. Piles of fajitas, guac, salsa and minced beef were inhaled, Sarah stuffing herself with the vegetarian alternative, a sort of medley of diced vegetables. Edward ended up with fajita sauce all round his mouth and down his chin, dribbling onto his shirt, and Lottie tutted and tried to dab at it with little success.

And they laughed. That was another unbreakable rule. You couldn't go round to Lottie's house without *fun*, leaving your problems at the front door and letting loose.

The meal was over as quickly as it had begun, the family sat around the table, nursing their swollen bellies. Lottie, Simon and Abe waited until the children had left to talk properly, shooing them away from the table and back upstairs into their bedrooms.

"What about pudding?" Sarah whined, eyeing the raspberry roulade, sat beneath a net on the side. "I'm not full yet, Mum!"

"Later," Lottie instructed, throwing a tea towel over the dessert and gesturing with her hands, flapping them about to make them leave. "Go on, the pair of you! We need some grown-up time, okay?"

She came back to the table with a dramatic sigh, and the three of them sat in silence for a moment, staring at the mess before them. There were plates and cutlery scattered everywhere, empty bowls showing the remnants of dips and coleslaw, a lonely carrot stick drifting in its dish.

"I better start washing up," Simon started, lifting from his seat, but Abe put out a hand to stop him.

"Can I say something first?" The other two nodded, so he added, "Because I need your help."

This was it.

This was what he'd been waiting for.

"What is it? Whatever it is, I told you we'd be happy to help –"

"It's not really about me," Abe cut in. The leg jiggling had returned, seat vibrating from the movement. "It's more... *complicated* than that."

"Then... what *is* it about?" Lottie frowned. "Is it about the kids?"

"No, no, nothing like that." He took a deep breath, pushing a hand down onto his leg to keep it still. The room grew silent around them, the vague sound of a toilet being flushed down the hallway ringing in his ears.

Another pause stretched on.

And then, "I... I want to find Patrick."

Lottie and Simon were quiet, staring at each other with parted mouths and wide eyes. Slowly, Lottie turned to Abe, shaking her head in disbelief.

"Patrick?" she repeated. "You're joking, aren't you? I haven't heard you mention his name in... what, *twenty years* or more."

"I know," Abe replied. He was blushing now, realising how daft it sounded, how stupid of an idea it was. "And I know it's probably a daft idea, he won't even remember me, but... I want to apologise. And if this doctor's right, then I better do it sooner, rather than later."

Lottie was still gobsmacked, her face the picture of shock. After Simon gave her wrist a pinch, she jerked her head slightly and stared at him, finally saying, "You... you want to apologise? To Patrick?"

Abe nodded, now feeling completely ridiculous. "I know it must sound crazy, but…"

"No, Abe." Slowly, Lottie stood and took deliberate steps over to him. Standing in front of him, her face broke into a huge, beaming smile. "I think it's the *best* idea you've had in a very long time."

At that moment, the door creaked open and a tiny head popped his head around it, letting out a yelp as it almost fell to the floor. All brown curls and huge, guilty eyes, Edward's bottom lip began to tremble as he insisted, "Sarah told me to eavesdrop!"

Another head came straight after, indignantly shaking. "I didn't, Mum, it was Edward's idea! I know it's bad to eavesdrop – is Edward going on the naughty list?"

"No, it was Sarah's idea! She eavesdrops on you and Dad all the time – that's how she knows about Patrick!"

"Oh, you *penguin*!" Sarah burst furiously. "Mum, Dad, I'm sorry, *please* still let me go to Santa's Christmas Ball this year, I beg you –"

"So you know about Patrick?" Abe cut in. There was a smile playing on his face, just a smidge, and the children detected it in an instant. "What do you think I should do? Find him and apologise, or…"

"Find him and apologise!" Edward said immediately. "That's what Sarah thinks too – she's been saying it for ages, ever since Aunt Mollie died."

"And we don't care that you're gay," Sarah added. "We both had an inkling when you got rid of all Aunt Mollie's pictures…"

"You little rats!" Lottie murmured, though she was smiling as she shook her head. "You knew this all along, and you didn't say anything?"

"You never tell us anything!" Sarah objected. "We knew you still wouldn't talk to us about it…"

"If they know that, they really *should* know everything," Abe said. Sarah and Edward frowned, cocking their heads in unison as they watched their Uncle Abe, and Lottie couldn't help but shrug, slumping into her chair with a sigh of defeat.

Abe turned back to the children. "I… I received some bad news today. I have an elfness. Incurable. I may only be around for a few more months."

Edward and Sarah didn't say a word, tiny mouths wobbling as they tried to absorb the news. The words were big, held magnitude; that, they sensed. But they didn't understand it, not fully, and wouldn't until he was gone – he knew that – and yet the three months resonated with both of them. Something inside each of them emphasised how *important* this was. They clutched hands tight and gazed back at Abe with identical wide brown eyes, a look of understanding on their faces.

"Okay," Sarah said, nodding. "Then we'll all help find Patrick for you, so you can say sorry."

"Thank you." Inside him, Abe could feel his heart swelling; it was indescribable, a feeling of warmth flooding his bones, his lungs, his fingers and toes. "Is everyone in?"

Simon looked nervous, unsure, and looked at Lottie for confirmation.

She was looking at her best friend, eyes narrowed, like she was trying to read him. This wasn't the Abe she knew and loved, but she wanted to love this new Abe. The Abe who was brave and bold and willing to take risks…

The Abe she'd wanted him to be for so, so long.

"I'm in," she said, face breaking into a smile. "Kids?"

"We're in!" came the echo from around the table, a collection of wide smiles and jerking heads in his direction, filling him with confidence.

"We'll find him, Uncle Abe," said little Edward, nodding his curly head. "I promise we will."

We could waste a lot of time talking about Abe's marriage to Mollie, dissecting the ways in which it might've turned out differently, in another life. We'll never know if Mollie truly loved Abe, what her intentions were in getting married. We'll never know if she wanted children, riches, success.

All we know is that she ended up a very happy woman, surrounded by friends and family, a best friend to Abe, too, in many ways… and Abe would always be grateful for that.

Mollie was your typical rich elf. She'd grown up under the umbrella of her daddy's business, never spent a penny of her own money in her life, and forged friendships and connections through her ruthlessness.

But in the end, it was the infertility which brought her crashing down to earth, showed her that she wasn't, in fact, invincible.

All she'd ever wanted was a little baby. Not love, not even fancy clothes or shoes, a pretty gingerbread handbag with a sugary gem clasp… but a baby, a tiny baby with a snub nose and blue eyes, all hers.

When the doctors gave them the news, it was her wakeup call, as it had been with Abe. A call to go out and have fun, find peace and happiness in all her life had to offer. She'd never been interested in romance - not even a little - and so she joined a craft club a week later, made a whole bunch of new friends. They bought a log cabin in the Jul Region between them, spent every January there for twenty years or more.

And she was content. She was content when she died on the sledge that day, tumbling over, snapping her neck.

In a world where so many are wanting, that's sometimes all you need.

NINETEEN

The next day, Abe and the others sat around Lottie's kitchen table as the sun came up, a notepad placed between them. The children were still in their pyjamas and Simon was supping coffee at the breakfast bar, nose red from the cold and breath coming out as smoke.

Abe frowned, flicking the pen across the shiny surface and watching as it spun in circles.

He had no idea where to begin.

It had been years since he'd done anything radical, anything new, anything just for him. Years of complying and conforming, years of going by their society's unspoken rules in order to live the life they expected of him, had turned him into the cold, unforgiving man he was today, the cranky old elf who still lived in the house he grew up in, who'd never moved anything, done anything different, made a *change*.

Lottie had fallen in love, of course, travelled the North Pole a little with her new husband and infants, before settling down. His own parents had joined clubs and groups in their short retirement, tried sports and new hobbies, given themselves goals.

Now, it was his turn.

"You'll need to find out where he lives," Sarah began,

poking Abe's arm with a tiny finger. "Then we can go and surprise him!"

"That's no good," Simon cut in. "You'll seem a little creepy, Abe – like you've stalked him. After the last time you saw him, you need to do this slowly, politely, make sure he consents to anything you do…"

The table fell silent for a moment, before Lottie spoke. "Are you sure you want to do this, Abe? It's just that… what if it doesn't go well? What if you spend your last months heartbroken, like you've gone back in time twenty, thirty years?"

Everyone flinched at the mention of his final months, but Abe was still. He was staring at his aged hands, his wizened fingers and the hairs which laced them, at the time they'd spent attached to his body, at how much they'd seen, how much they'd done… and at how much of that was involuntary.

He didn't want to rekindle things with Patrick… not now, not this late. He only needed closure. For him to accept an apology, or agree to be friends, or even just shake his hand and tell him that he was *sorry*, that he knew Abe had messed up but that it was all in the past now, they could move on and forget all about it.

"I'll be okay," he said suddenly, nodding his head. He glanced up to meet the eyes of his family, and four pairs stared back, crinkled and smiling at the weight of his words, the strength of his decision. "I need to do this. I need to do what I should've done thirty sodding years ago, Lotts."

Lotts.

A nickname he scarcely used now, especially in times like these, one which had died out when happiness disappeared, when they married and grew older and stopped being best friends. Now, they were more like siblings to one another. The siblings they'd never had.

She was blinking back tears now as she reached out to grasp his hand. "You can't think like that, Abe, or you'll never stop beating yourself up about it."

"I *deserve* to beat myself up about it," he retorted, banging his fist against the table for effect. It was too weak, and the wood beneath him barely trembled. An embarrassment. "I've spent the last thirty years regretting that day, and it's taken a blooming elfness diagnosis, a dead wife and me selling the business to actually do anything. I just…"

"You can't change that now, Uncle Abe." The voice came from little Edward now, gazing up at his uncle with wide eyes and an expression which screamed innocence. "My teacher always says that you can't change the past, only the future. Whenever any of the other boys pick on me, she always tells me that I can't take back what they've done, but they can alter what'll happen in the future by apologising and promising not to do it again."

Abe sighed, and couldn't help but reach out to ruffle his head. Smiling weakly at the boy who wasn't really his nephew but in every sense that mattered *was*, he turned to the others with a nod.

"Wise words from our very own Edward," he said, once again banging the table with his fist. This time, however, it ricocheted around the room, rattling the windows in their refurbed frames and shaking the walls, the shelves, Abe's entire body. Courage surged through him, reignited once again. "We need a plan, ladies and gentlemen. We need a *good* plan."

***

In the end, they spent the next three hours brainstorming at the kitchen table. Sugar paper sheets covered the wood surface as they scribbled and drew and wrote and sketched, imagining what Patrick would look like now, how tall he'd be, whether he'd have a beard, long hair, what job he might be doing.

They came up with ideas for where they might find him, drawing on locations in the Natale Region, the shop on Tinsel Street, his grandparents' cottage in the Jul Region, the kids tasked with drawing each location and both Patrick and Abe within them, little tongues stuck out in concentration.

Once every idea had been pulled from their minds and scattered across the page, they sat back to admire their handy work. Lottie and Simon were beaming proudly, the children giggling at each other's depictions of their uncle, and Abe simply sat there, silent, as he took in the sheet, all the places, the names, Patrick's face, looming from the paper, those huge brown eyes and fingers, like cookie dough, emerging from a puffer jacket with a fluffy head.

"I'm blooming lucky to have friends like you," he said, out of nowhere. The others just stared back, a little taken aback, as Abe's eyes followed the line of the page, the writing, each word.

"We're not just friends," Lottie said, after a pause. "We're family."

"Pot-ay-toe, pot-ah-toe." Abe shook his head, scouring the table again and reaching to pull the children into a hug. They nestled into him, their old, frail Uncle Abe, filling his nostrils with their childish scent, one of candy canes and strawberry laces. "You don't have to help me, though. You're... you're good, decent people."

"As are you," Lottie replied. "Which is *why* we have to help you."

Abe couldn't argue with that.

Lottie waited years to have a baby. Mollie, now a firm acquaintance and trustee, told her not to; that it would be more dangerous the longer she waited, that she should be lucky she was so healthy, young.

But Lottie wanted more. She expanded her business, grew it from a tiny pâtisserie to a line of fancy bakeries across the North Pole, with a store even in the Natale Region, near where Patrick lived.

Little did he know that one of the waitresses there, serving the people of the region pastries and tarts in pastel pink paper, was Betsy, Patrick's little sister, now all grown up, working a full-time job to support her boyfriend and their little baby boy.

Lottie had travelled, too, searching all over the North Pole for elves who could supply her the finest ingredients… creamy Wensleydale cheese with ginger and cranberries, a selection of chutneys from a small town called Vibbington, in Europe somewhere. Gin made with nutmeg and juniper, delicious strands of turmeric and slices of free range turkey. She made a lot of money, in her short life. Now that she was thinking about settling down, taking on more managers, she had a legacy, family to pass her business on to, staff who she knew could be trusted to take it over if not.

Lottie had been brave. She'd always known, in her heart, what she wanted.

She wanted peace, and she wanted to make delicious pastries.

But she also wanted love.

She'd found that, all right. Now, she had two children. Sarah was her firstborn, headstrong and determined, Edward her shadow, looking up to Sarah in the way Lottie had always looked up to Abe. She was grateful that he'd always have a sister to guide him.

Just like Abe.

TWENTY

The first port of call was Natale Regional Council, which had a tiny office at the edge of the town. Lottie took Abe in a cab they'd hired, buzzing with excitement and with bright red cheeks as they drove through the snowy December streets, cloaked and wearing thick hats and gloves as the weather battled around them. Simon and the kids waved them off from the doorstep, before he bustled them inside, away from the cold.

Lottie sat back in her seat, beaming ecstatically. Despite the chill, there was a feverish energy around them, rabid and intense.

"Do you know what you're going to say?" she asked, eyes wide. "If we find him, that is."

"I thought I'd be spontaneous," Abe replied drolly. "Turn on my famous charm…"

Yet as the office grew nearer and the streets became darker, soot-stained factories lining the roads and bedraggled tinsel hanging from lampposts, Abe felt his heart begin to race and his throat grow constructed, withered lungs straining in an effort to breathe in the smoggy air. It wasn't a game anymore, a bit of fun that seemed exciting, entertaining. This was real life. Now that the kids weren't here to make light of it, he had a sudden feeling of free-falling – he had *no idea* what he was doing.

They turned down a backstreet and the cab pulled to a stop. The driver frowned as he watched them disembark, holding a hand out for his payment.

"We'll be wanting a lift back very soon, if you could wait," Lottie suggested as she passed him some coins, but he was already trotting away down the road, even the horse spluttering in the smoky air. The pair huddled together, cold buzzing around them like a swarm of jabbing flies, thick and icy, wading through the slush.

"Come on," Lottie said, holding a hand over her mouth. "The sooner we get inside, the better."

It was a tiny building, made of dirty red brick and tacky plastic doors, which were stationed at the top of a ramp. The railing was bright yellow and garish, and soggy white clouds hung above them, just visible through the air. There was a dank smell all around the office, curling between their bodies and tickling their nostrils.

"It reeks of sewage," Lottie spluttered, pinching her nose with her other hand. "Oh my *baubles*, Abe, can you smell that?"

But Abe was despondent, staring up at the office with narrowed eyes. He didn't say anything, but began to walk up the ramp on steady feet, one before the other, walking stick clutched tight beneath a withered hand.

"Stay there," he instructed, turning his head to view his best friend for one last time. "I need to do this on my own."

He pushed through the double doors and a bell tinkled above, alerting the sleepy receptionist of his arrival. She had pointed ears sticking out from a head of thick, straw-like blonde hair, a typical elfish smile curved above her sharp chin. Around them, dismal decorations hung against peeling wallpaper, the floor a horrible shade of forest green, laced with stains and patches of trodden gum.

"Good morning!" she said, immediately digging her quill into a pot of ink and preparing herself to begin writing. "How can I help you today?"

"I'm trying to find someone," Abe said, resting his stick against the desk. He didn't want to show that he was out of breath – he didn't want pity – and so kept his mouth closed and tried to inhale through his nose, chest wheezing inside of him at a rate of knots. "They live in the Natale Region, see, and…"

"Ah," the receptionist said, frowning. "Now, if you want personal details about someone in the area, you need proof that you knew them."

"Proof?" Abe repeated. He could feel his stomach begin to sink as he stared at her, exasperated. "I don't have proof! If I had proof, I wouldn't need to find him, would I?"

"Who exactly is it that you're trying to find?" she asked. "A long lost cousin, a girlfriend, old colleague…"

"My ex-boyfriend," Abe said flatly. "Patrick."

That's when the receptionist looked at him – *really* looked at him – and let out a gasp of shock.

"Abe?" she whispered. "You're… you're Abraham Cane!"

And that's when it clicked.

"Dora?" Abe murmured, realisation dawning within him. The scrawny elf before him, with her sharp little face and animated expressions, a 'D' necklace hung around her neck…

How had he not realised sooner? Dora, Patrick's best friend and ex-girlfriend, a waitress at the Gingerbread Restaurant, sat here in front him, before his very eyes.

"I never expected to see you again!" she said, shaking her

head. Both of her hands were trembling against the edge of the desk. "After you were a complete *dick* and broke his heart, we assumed you'd be smart and stay away."

"I was twenty. I didn't know what I was doing –"

But Dora wasn't listening, talking at a rate of knots and stumbling over her words. "And now that Patrick has Michael, we assumed he wouldn't need to see you again, either."

"Patrick..." Abe's words trailed off as his stomach dipped even lower, right to his bowels. "He has a partner?"

"A partner, yes." Dora rolled her eyes, standing up from behind her desk so as to stand face to face. "They got together a few years after he met you, actually."

Abe didn't know what to say. It was like his body was malfunctioning beneath him, but inside, he was numb.

"So you've had a wasted journey, Abe," she continued. "Even if Patrick wanted to see you, we wouldn't let him – you're no good for him. You'll only end up breaking his heart again."

But Abe was barely listening. It was like his brain had turned to ice, impenetrable beneath the walls of his skull. He turned to leave, grabbing his stick and walking slowly towards the door, but a hand grabbed his arm and jerked him backwards with a sharp tug.

"Why did you want to see him, Abe?" Dora was watching him carefully with those inquisitive eyes, sharp chin poised. Abe went to speak, frowning – and yet hesitated.

Why *did* he want to see Patrick?

Was it because he missed him, or because he felt guilty?

Was it because he wanted Patrick to know how sorry he was, how awful he still felt about humiliating him at Santa's Christmas Ball?

Or was it just because he was selfish and lonely and sad, and he knew, deep down, that was the last chance he'd ever get to make it up to him before he died?

"I have an elfness," he said finally. "The doctor's given me three months to live. I just... I never meant to hurt him, Dora, you *must* know that. I was twenty and confused and lost, but I never would have deliberately put him through that pain."

Around them, the room groaned. The light to the centre of the ceiling flickered on and off, on and off, the first time Abe had noticed its faulty tendencies since walking through the door.

But Dora was smiling, a mischievous smirk that lit up her face.

"That's what Patrick said, you know. That you'd never meant to hurt him. I guess part of me thought he was just making up excuses, but... you really loved him, didn't you? That's why we thought it was so out of character when you..."

"I did love him," Abe admitted. "I just need to see him, Dora. I can't explain why, not really. I don't know myself."

"Then let's find him for you," she replied, grinning. "And if you break him again, I'll break you. Deal?"

Abe nodded. "Deal."

***

Lottie's eyes almost popped from her sockets when she saw Dora progressing down the ramp towards them, now wrapped in a scarf, coat and bobble hat to protect herself from the cold. It was raining, a sleet-like kind of precipitation, dripping from damp clouds and soaking them to the bone.

"There's no point getting a cab. It's only a few streets away."

They walked mainly in silence, shielded from the cold with umbrellas held high above their heads, catching the rain. Abe wandered a little behind, chest straining at the effort of lifting both feet as he tried to make his stick steady on the slimy floor, afraid of slipping and falling right over onto the pavement. Lottie tried to engage Dora in conversation, but she was more interested in checking as they crossed roads and avoided potholes, stepping round manure.

"Are you married?" Lottie asked politely, as they turned the corner onto another backstreet, even darker and denser than the last.

"David and I got together shortly after Pat and Mike," Dora replied distractedly, twisting her head from side to side. A bedraggled line of tinsel lay across the pavement, which they stepped over carefully. David. Patrick's other best friend. Abe had always secretly assumed that he was also in love with Patrick, and that that was why he was so protective of him. Clearly not. "We have four kids, which is a bit of a nightmare, but contraception isn't a viable option for us… I just found out I'm pregnant again, so whoop-ee. I thought I was too old, but I guess not."

They turned off onto another road, this one so much narrower, the large gates of a factory perched at one end. Abe frowned as he recognised the name on the gates, the familiar blue and white logo sending off signals in his mind.

"Wait – that's the snowball factory!" he exclaimed, banging his stick against the tarmac. "I knew I recognised the logo! Wow, it's *huge*. The people who live down this road must never stop eating them!"

"If they could afford excessive snowballs, I'm sure that'd

be the case," Dora cut in sharply. "Sadly, it's only middle-class buffoons who buy them – no one round here would waste much of their hard-earned cash on salted crap."

That told them.

There was a house right at the end of the road, narrower than the rest, with metal bars on the windows. It looked like it had once been white, but the soot and smoke had stained it dark grey, patches of dead ice clinging limply to areas of exposed brick. On the step were two bottles of milk on a tiny tray, left out from the milkman's early morning visit.

"They mustn't be up yet," Dora observed, frowning. "Don't worry, you can wait at mine in the meantime – unless you have something to get back for?"

"We can wait!" Lottie tugged on Abe's arm, gesturing to the house. While Dora's back was turned, she mouthed, "Why are there bars on the windows?"

Dora unlocked the door to her own terraced house, which was just next door, the same fading colour and yet looked after, cleaner, the windows brightly scrubbed and tiny square of front garden neatly clipped into place. The front hall was sparsely furnished and smelt of Irish cream, and she led them through into the cramped front room. It was full of colour and blankets, mismatched cushions on every chair and assorted toys scattered across the floor.

"The three babies are at nursery, and Marley's at school – yet this is *still* the state of our front room." She gestured for them to take a seat, then moved over towards the door. "I'll be right back, so please, make yourselves at home!"

The minute she was gone, Lottie let out a huge sigh of relief and flopped back against the chair. She turned to Abe with a shaking head and picked up one of the cushions between her thumb and forefinger. "This whole place is covered in dog hairs! How is she comfortable, letting her kids play with toys covered in dog slobber? And where did she even get all of these bedraggled teddies from, do you think? They look so…"

"Dirty?" Abe raised an eyebrow. He could hardly stand to look around the room; it made him feel so *sick*. It was baffling, how little they could afford, yet the way they just *made do* with it all. The mismatched cushions, second-hand toys, chewed-up dog bowl in the corner… it was a house that had been crafted from personality and love, and yet the lingering scent and hair-covered surfaces told the truth about its background. "It makes you feel guilty, doesn't it? We have so much tat, and they're living like… well, like this."

"It's not our fault," Lotte responded. "We can't *help* being more fortunate than them."

"We could do more to help," he cut in. "Everyone could. They can't even get a proper education here, Lotts, and yet we look down on them for being poor."

"Again, not our fault," Lottie reasoned. "Or our problem."

"Then maybe that's the issue."

Lottie frowned, misunderstanding. "Tell *that* to Nick St. Clair."

They were silent for a minute or two, refusing to glance up to meet each other's eyes. A fake Christmas tree sat in the opposite corner to the dog bowl, where a TV would traditionally go. It was leaning slightly with the weight of homemade Christmas decorations and misplaced tinsel, and one or two rather depressing looking parcels sat beneath its lower boughs, dumpy and forlorn.

The door creaked open then, and Abe glanced up. Dora was at the door, cheeks red from the cold, beckoning to him with one finger.

"Patrick wants to see you, Abe," she said. "He's waiting outside now, with a cab."

Every air on Abe's body seemed to stand still, coming to a halt as he sat stiffly on the sofa, staring forwards with his heart in his mouth.

"Are you sure?" he asked, voice hoarse. "I – I – I really don't know what I'm doing, you know."

"Apologising," Dora replied. "Now go on – you're not allowed to let him down again, remember?"

But letting Patrick down was the last thing Abe ever wanted to do again.

"*Baubles*," he breathed softly. "I'm really doing this."

"Yeah," Lottie added. "You really are."

He glanced up to meet her eyes and was greeted by a wide, brown eyed smile, staring right back at him.

"You've got this, Abe," she whispered. "I promise."

He wasn't entirely sure if he believed her.

You might be wondering how on earth it came to be that Patrick found love after the heartbreak of Abraham Cane… but that really would be telling.

All you really need to know is one simple fact.

Because no matter how hard the first love hits, there's no reason the second shouldn't hit just as fiercely.

Patrick and Michael were the kind of couple you aspire to be by the time you reach your twenties, maybe even your thirties, and start thinking about settling down. No kids, a few cats, a small house, cosy. Saving up to spend your weekends off in the cottage in the mountains your grandparents left your family, rented out for a bit of extra money.

Patrick's mum lived in a similar cottage now, nearer to the Noël Region. She liked Michael - liked Michael a lot. They visited her most days, taking food and kisses and happiness, and played board games around the fire.

They had more than just a classic Monopoly board now. Betsy bought the family a new game every year, always winning now, older, wiser, pretty, still just as eager to be like her older brother.

Patrick and Michael were warm, cosy, comfortable. They might not have been as passionately in love as Patrick had been with Abe… but they weren't twenty anymore.

They were fifty-one, older, wiser. Happy.

They made the most of every second they had left, aware of how precious life was.

They never took that for granted.

TWENTY-ONE

There was a man on the doorstep as Abe stepped outside. A man he didn't know, didn't recognise, but who was staring at Abe with such venom that the ignorance definitely wasn't mutual.

"I'm Michael," he said quickly, holding out a hand for Abe to shake. "Michael Solstice."

Michael – Patrick's new partner.

He was squat and uncomfortable looking, with a bushy gingery beard and awkward spectacles, perched across the end of his nose and staring up at Abe. He was a good ten centimetres shorter, too; with beady green eyes like lightbulbs. He was probably Patrick's height, maybe a little less, and built like him, too, soft, warm. Abe blushed as he shook the hand back. He glanced up briefly to scour the street, noticing a cab sat a few houses away. Its contents were turned away from him, hidden.

"I wanted to introduce myself before you… you know." Michael shifted on his feet, eyes flickering up to follow Abe's line of vision. "Patrick and I have been together for nearly thirty years, Abraham. I know what happened between you two was intense, but I can't let you take him from me now. I just – I just – I *can't*."

Abe raised an eyebrow and leaned further down on his stick, feeling a cough rise in his throat.

This man – this weird, speccy man, stood before him like a trembling leaf – was clearly so threatened by him that it almost incited *pride*.

He'd never really been *threatening* before to anybody before. He'd gotten angrier over the last few years, obviously, maybe a little more aggressive, but he didn't see enough people to put said aggression into practice.

He swallowed now, determined not to let his elfness show, and cocked his head to one side.

"Why would I do that?" he asked, voice lingering on scornful.

Michael shuddered. "Because I've never lived up to his expectations – *never*. It was always you he was comparing me to. You, his first love, the person he actually wanted to be with. I was always just a reserve. We've got so much planned, so much to do once we retire in a few years, and I can't let you ruin it for us!"

"I'm just going to apologise to him," Abe said. "That's all."

"Yes, well…" Michael shifted awkwardly and flapped at his collar, as if struggling for air. "Because if you try anything on, I'll – I'll –"

"You'll whack me one?" Abe suggested. "You'll give me a piece of your mind?"

"Yes!" Michael responded, nodding. "Yes, yes, yes to all of that!"

The cab had begun to move slowly down the road towards them, moving backwards in an unnerving, ghostly fashion, through the smog. It was a black hansom pulled by a brown-spotted horse, the kind you'd never, ever encounter in the Noël Region, and Abe's heart was in his mouth as he watched it, hands clutched tight against the head of his walking stick as it progressed further.

"So don't do anything you'll live to regret," Michael was saying, shaking his fist in a somewhat menacing manner. "Don't you dare!"

Trying to appear like he wasn't limping, Abe started walking down the path to the road. He could scarcely breathe, and not just because of the elfness; the lump of anxiety lodged in his throat was swelling, taking over his trachea and exploding over the inside of his mouth in what he hoped wouldn't be a bout of verbal diarrhoea –

His lungs ached with cold, lips chapped and sore, feet dragging as he made his way towards the cab. The pavement wasn't the teeniest bit even and he struggled to keep upright as he made his way down it.

"Sod this," he muttered to himself, mostly just to ease the anxiety, which was building up inside of him, creeping up and out of his mouth.

The cab had stopped right in front of him, the head of its passenger still turned away from him. All Abe could see was a scarcely covered, light brown scalp, covered in freckles, the neck rolling together into a pair of soft lips. Pulling himself up onto the seat took every bit of effort he could muster, and his lungs were screaming as he landed, hands red raw and painful.

The head still didn't move, completely stationary, staring out of the other window, to the opposite side of the road. Abe tried to arrange himself in the seat, but his body was in too much pain, arms aching, backside stiff.

"Patrick," he said, voice hoarse.

The head slowly turned around.

The eyes... it was the eyes. Abe felt a sudden explosion of

pain in his chest and doubled over, tears swelling as those huge, melted-chocolate irises repeated over and over in his mind. A hand on his shoulder, soft, and two fingers gently pressed against the edge of his collarbone; warm breath against his face, hot and sticky, like syrup; and those eyes, those wonderful eyes he'd missed so much, cushioned against his like hot cocoa slipping all over his body.

"Abraham," Patrick murmured, shaking his head gently. "Abraham Cane."

***

The cab began to trot away down the road, but the two of them stayed in the same position, huddled close on the back seat. Abe's withered hands clutched the stick tight as Patrick stared at him, taking in his bushy eyebrows, bald head, discoloured freckles.

And Patrick… he looked exactly like Abe had expected. He was more in shape now, the thick arms more toned than chubby, face covered in eager stubble. His dark eyebrows were neat and trimmed, not a single hair between them, and he was dressed in a fine felt coat and checked scarf. He looked… sophisticated. Older, more mature, like he'd grown into himself, shifted from a boy to a man over the last thirty years and yet somehow stayed exactly the *same*.

He also seemed so much more comfortable, if that was possible. He'd always been brave, owned who he was, but his personality shone now. He looked *proud*, somehow. Confident. Like he knew exactly who he was, and wouldn't change that for the world.

"You don't look well," was the first thing Patrick pointed out, frowning. He took in Abe's face, body, withered lungs, the way he stooped, eyelids saggy and puffed out, nose quivering with dripping snot.

It didn't surprise Abe that this had happened straight away; that Patrick had noticed something was wrong. No matter how much chemistry was sizzling between them, how much history and forgotten feelings left unsaid...

His elfness hung between them like a big black cloud, the elephant in the room brought from the corner almost immediately.

Abe took a deep breath. It didn't really matter if he told him; after all, that was why he was here. To apologise to Patrick, and to say sorry, after all of these years.

To get closure, but also to become *friends* once more, rekindle some sort of relationship between them.

And in order to do that, he needed to tell the truth.

"It's an elfness," he said, after a pause. "I'm in the late stages. It's spread around my body."

Silence fell around them, shellshocked on Patrick's behalf, tense and in waiting on Abe's. They were just pulling clear of the Natale Region and so the streets were cleaner, brighter, the sleet still falling like tiny bullets around them.

"An elfness," Patrick echoed, leaning back and blinking several times, as though to try and absorb the information. "How long do you have left?"

It was a brutal question, but they both knew it was the reason Abe had requested to see him; that was obvious. No one ever recovered from elfnesses, whatever the kind, wherever they sat in the body. The urgency of the situation was stark between them.

"Three months."

Silence once again enveloped them, this time painful and red, too raw for either of them to cope with. Abe rubbed his withered knuckles as the sleet turned to rain, tiny bullets of water shooting from the sky at a rate of knots. The snow seemed to disappear around them as the droplets splattered it into oblivion. It was cold, achingly so, and Abe was greatly regretting his outfit choice. His skinny wrists hung out of his coat sleeves and led to frozen hands, bright vermillion and stinging.

The Noël Region blossomed around them as their cab pulled down the street, all brightly coloured shops and fresh produce, butcher's and baker's and greengrocer's, dripping from the sudden shower. Lights still shone and left smatterings of joy across puddles, piles of slush laying here and there against the edges of the road.

But Patrick was subdued, staring out at the passing buildings with a straight face.

"There's your shop," he pointed out flatly. He screwed up his eyes to stare as it as they passed, adding, "Wait… it says Dotty's Doughnuts now. What happened there?"

"I sold it." Abe faked a smile, glancing sidewards at Patrick. "To fund my retirement. Which is going outstandingly well, if I do say so myself."

Patrick couldn't help but smirk at that – not at the subject, but at Abe's dry humour, the bluntness of his statement. "So you never carried on the business anyway? I bet your parents were pretty annoyed."

"Mollie and I couldn't have kids," Abe cut in. It still stung to say her name out loud. He could see Patrick flinch as the words left his mouth, but Abe continued regardless, shivering at the very thought of his late wife. "They tried to make me get an apprentice to carry on the business, but I think the whole thing kind of ran its course. There's no market for repairing things anymore – consumerism, you know?"

"So... you married her? The girl from Santa's Ball?" Patrick asked, completely disregarding the last statement. He was looking at Abe curiously as he waited for an answer.

"I was young, confused," he said, shaking his head. "You know how it is, Patrick, especially in the Noël Region. And... I loved her, in my own way. We had a friendship, a mutual partnership. It wasn't all bad."

"I get it."

They were silent again, as the horse trotted on and the Noël Region faded around them. The turn-off for Tinsel Street was fast approaching as Patrick reached to put a hand on the driver's shoulder, saying, "Could you let us out here?"

They slowed to a stop, Patrick helping Abe down the steps. He held the stick as they descended, passing it back with an awkward smile as they stepped onto the street and across the cobbles, wandering at Abe's slower pace as they found their footing and progressed down the road.

It had almost stopped raining now, pinpricks of water dripping from the sky like gems, and there weren't many shoppers about; the street was almost empty, shop doors closed to keep out the cold and stall owners shivering under their canopies in six hundred layers.

On Tinsel Street, it was easy to forget your every worry, to just *exist*.

Abe opened his wallet to buy them both a hot dog, topping each with stuffing and cranberry sauce, the sausage meat herby and Cumberland, imported straight from the British countryside in time for Christmas. They drank coffee from a little paper cup, laughing as Patrick got cream all over his nose, and – for the first time in months – Abe didn't feel ill or old or tired. He just felt happy, more than he'd felt in a long time.

It was strange, how quickly they'd sunk back into that rhythm, the old familiarity which had once made it so easy to fall in love... and as quickly as they had, too. It felt as though they'd never been apart, hadn't spent years separated by time and space and status, hadn't come from completely different places, different backgrounds, worlds away from one another.

Soulmates, Abe was thinking, the word twisting over and over in his mind as he wandered down the familiar street, one he'd passed so many times with Mollie, with Lottie, with Simon and the kids... and with Patrick, all those years ago, hand in hand, falling in love.

Little did he know, Patrick was thinking the exact same thing.

I'll let you in on a little secret, if you insist.

In the North Pole, elves aren't meant to live forever. Life has always been intended to end. What would be the point in living a long, happy life, and letting it hang longer than necessary? We need fresh blood, fresh meat.

It's a cycle, you see.

Elves must die to make way for new elves, new ideas, to keep the Christmas spirit strong, alive. Not that elves ever really die. They simply wither away, bit by bit, until they become just another star in the sky.

So when you next look up into at the stars, see those pinpricks of light poking through the atmosphere, think of all those little elves who had to die to make a beautiful canopy above you.

There are rumours about these elfnesses.

Some say they're caused by the decaying of the spirit, that they can hit at random, that no one ever really knows when their body will start to disperse, turn to dust.

Others say they're a cause of poor diet; though anyone eating mince pies and cranberry sauce for all snacks and meals will, undoubtedly, put a stopper on their life eventually.

But most, collectively, agree that elfnesses are brought on by a lack of Christmas spirit.

That if elves don't embrace the festivities enough, their body will start to give up, to collapse, just like that.

That the Christmas spirit is the only thing fuelling each elf, turning their little legs to wheels, turning round and round and round in the snow.

Over the years, Abe had definitely fallen out of love with Christmas.

It happens to so many of us. We start to see it as a time of spending, of fancy presents and dressing up and eating expensive food, when that's really not what Christmas is all about. Whether you're religious or simply believe in Santa and his rein-

-deers, the collection of elves buzzing around his magical land, Christmas is about a feeling, a fizz.

It's the sparkle in your stomach as you put homemade decorations on trees, dressed in your funny little Father Christmas hat, hanging stockings on the fireplace, stitched with your initials, by hand.

It's eating gingerbread, hot from the oven, and walking home in the snow from school, eyes watering, wanting nothing more than to catch a piece of the magic and bottle it forever.

It's closing your eyes and wishing on a star, placing a carrot out for Rudolph, swallowing your turkey quickly because it's actually not that nice, because you prefer chicken. It's hugging your grandparents and kissing them on the cheek, keeping every single card from your mum, with its biro scribbled xxx.

It's love, and it's understanding.

Forgiveness.

Peace.

But Abe was finding this out all too late.

TWENTY-TWO

The turnoff for the Gingerbread Restaurant sprung upon Abe. As Patrick started to lead him down the path and away from Tinsel Street, he paused to catch his breath, wheezing as he clung to his friend's arm.

"My late wife – Mollie – her family used to run the place." His voice was all off kilter as he tried to explain, jabbing his arm at the alley ahead. "She sold it when she inherited it twenty years ago, and we haven't been back since."

Patrick blinked at him for a second, then repeated, as though he'd misheard, "She inherited the Gingerbread Restaurant and *sold it?*"

"My business made enough money to keep us afloat." Patrick's expression was still incredulous as Abe explained, straightening up as he tried to regulate his breathing, get a proper grasp of his cane. "Mollie wasn't much of a businesswoman, see. She… she liked nice things, clothes, shoes, handbags, that sort of thing. Running a restaurant wasn't really her style."

"I think I need to know more about this late wife of yours, Abraham."

The path was more trodden than it had been thirty years ago, when the pair had wandered over fresh snow in their mules and almost slipped over on patches of newly frosted ice. The walls of the shops on either side were damp with mildew, paint peeling; the magic of the Noël Region, the spectacle which was once the most sought after area in all of the North Pole, had faded, drifted, since they first fell in love.

Not all of it was ruined, however.

As they turned the corner and emerged from the darkness, that familiar plain of white appeared, behind Tinsel Street and surrounded by trees, branches, sparse shrubbery. It looked so different in broad daylight, of course, though the sky was clouded and snow was threatening, but the field they'd stumbled across that first evening was still the same expanse, waiting for footsteps, for Abe and Patrick to cross it, to make their mark.

Abe was slow, of course, but Patrick helped him, helped him all the way across the field and towards the trees, where the copse gave way to the archway of lights, of candles and tiny bulbs and magical flames, flickering as they ducked through it. The light shone warm white as they made their way through the tunnel, under the woven stars… and there it was. The Gingerbread Restaurant, rising from the snow in all its baked glory, beaming at the two men as they walked towards it.

"It's just as beautiful as I remember," Patrick said, eyes wide, drinking in the sight, the house crafted entirely out of gingerbread, held into place using the magic of the North Pole.

And it truly was magical, stood there beneath the trees, surrounded by a winter wonderland. Abe's breath was held, hands clutching his stick, knees wobbling as he stared.

Since Mollie had sold the place all those years ago, the Gingerbread Restaurant had only got bigger, better, more impressive, filled with the essence of Christmas it had once profited from so obtusely. The windows were now paned not with colourful sugar-glazed glass, but with tasteful white, frosted and patterned with snowflakes; the gems on the walls outside were colour-coordinated, rather than the traditional red and green they'd once used; the door, framework and lattice were all pale blue, like a winter sky, crafted from careful chocolate and made to last.

They didn't move for a moment, simply looking all around them and taking it in, feeling the festivity wash over them, fill them from head to toe with joy, with wonder, with the feeling they'd once labelled happiness.

That was enough for now.

"Shall we?" Patrick said, grabbing Abe's arm to pull him forwards.

Abe could do nothing but oblige.

They only had to knock twice before an elf answered the door, dressed just as Dora had done all those years ago, when she'd waitressed here. Fake freckles dark and pointed ears erect, the elf took Abe's stick with one swift movement and led them to their table, dropping them on each seat with a bow of her head.

"Menus," she said, as two appeared in the air beside them, and the pair were instructed to grab them, to bring them down to earth.

"This place has changed," Patrick said with a smirk, taking hold of his menu and yanking it onto the tabletop with a grunt. "I'm not sure I fully approve…"

Starters lined the first page, accompanied with dinky illustrations and perfect drawings of cheeses and meats and olives of all different colours, sizes. The restaurant was bustling with life around them, with kids and teens and couples on dates, just like Abe and Patrick had been, aged twenty and with their whole lives stretched out ahead. They were mainly boy-girl couples, but two girls sat together on the opposite side of the room, by the window, hands intertwined on the table in front of them, beaming and giggling at one another.

They were the lucky ones, Abe thought, staring at them, at their happy faces and bright smiles. Lucky that they could be here, together, without a care in the world, without the judgement of their family and friends and community. They must have accepting parents, he decided, or else they wouldn't be here, picking at a Christmassy sundae and playing with each other's pointed ears, the North Pole on their side.

Or maybe times had simply... changed. Abe wasn't sure.

He had no time for the present, as he was still so stuck in the past.

Patrick ordered the starters. Abe had already made his mind up on the fact he was going to pay; after seeing Patrick's house and its state of squalor, he couldn't stomach halving the bill, letting him use up any of his hard-earned cash on a day *he'd* arranged. Patrick was clearly hesitant with prices, going for the lesser option, until Abe stepped in and picked three more items off the menu, nudging Patrick with his foot.

"My treat."

The food arrived in the nick of time, appearing before them on the table as their waitress materialised, beaming. She held out her hand to present the cutlery, and Patrick and Abe took a bundle each, smiling shyly at one another beneath her gaze.

The food was incredible, of course – it hadn't changed in twenty years, hadn't downgraded in thirty. Baked camembert bites with a garlic dip; olives on sticks, stuffed with festive chilli peppers and mixed spice; honey-glazed parsnip fingers; smoked salmon, folded over crackers of rosemary and chive, just the right amount of crisp.

The mains came next. A giant beef Wellington, a layer of turkey separating the beef and pastry, mint sauce and redcurrant jelly and crisp roast potatoes adorning the pot. Carrots and peas and turnip slathered in butter and herbs, and a side of celeriac, creamed into a purée.

And cocktails, of course, now that they were well overage and experienced in matters of the world. A Christmas Pornstar Martini, and a virgin Bloody Mary for Patrick, who wasn't the biggest drinker. Soft fruit lined the glasses and sugar clung to the edges, decorating their lips as they took their first sips.

But desserts, of course, were a highlight of the Gingerbread Restaurant, an establishment made entirely from sweets.

They ordered a little bit of everything, Christmas-tinted cuisine from around the globe, inspired by Santa's travels each Christmas Eve. Delightful salted caramel mochi, stretchy and soft and melt-in-the-mouth; strawberry tarts with coconut and guava ice cream; pastries from France, covered in sultanas and sugar and crumbly against the palette; Chinese mooncakes, decorated with candy canes and drizzled in chocolate; cinnamon barfi, sweet and tender and oozy all at once.

They ate and ate and ate, like they had done all those years ago – and they talked. They talked about Mollie, about Patrick's new partner Michael, about Dora and David getting together and all their kids, and about Lottie and her husband, Abe's new family.

They skirted round the elfness, of course. It was left in the corner of the restaurant, where Abe's stick was going cold by the coat stand.

But besides all of that – besides the elfness, their new partners, the way life had changed, the bad blood running deep between them – they laughed. They laughed until their bellies ached and their sides hurt from great, rumbling huffs, on and on and on, into the afternoon.

After all…

They were still Patrick and Abe.

And now for Dora and David…

Dora and David had only been together twenty-five years or so, and had waited a while before deciding to have children. They had a happy relationship... the kind that comes from real love. They'd been best friends for so long that the transition felt odd, unnatural. When Dora asked David out for drinks one night, biting her lip and rubbing her straw-coloured hair with her hand, he almost lost his hat in shock.

"I… you want to go out for drinks?"

"Yes."

"But… you mean with Patrick, right?"

"He's busy tonight."

"So… is this a…"

"A date?"

"I… yeah, I guess so."

"You could call it that."

A pause.

"Do you want it to be a date, David?"

"If you want it to be a date, Dora."

They went out for cocktails, forking out for two each, though Dora paid, over the moon with her new promotion to receptionist at the council offices. She'd previously been a sort of secretary, writing up reports in green ink, ticking boxes in red. It still wouldn't bring in the millions, but it was enough.

It was a cold night – it was the North Pole, after all – and David offered Dora his jacket, tucking it around her shoulders with a small smile.

"Tonight was fun," Dora said, pulling it further over her chest, shivering. Her lips were blue and she was dressed in a light dress suit from her day at work, and David was striding along in a white shirt, forearms bare, looking as gorgeous as he always had done to Dora.

"We should do it again," David said, nodding. He turned to her, eyes going all melty and round, and said, "I… I should've asked you out earlier, Dora.

I'm not sure what's wrong with me. I suppose a part of me always thought you still wanted Pat."

Dora wrinkled her nose. "I don't think I ever really wanted Pat like that. I wasn't sure what I wanted, then."

Dora had had a few boyfriends since, but nothing serious.

She'd always hoped David would ask her out, just to see if it could work between them, if the spark was all in her head. When it didn't, she took matters into her own hands.

And thank goodness she did.

"I've liked you for ages, by the way," she said, nudging him sheepishly with her toe. "I though you might have noticed."

David, eyes wide, turned to look at her. "Notice? Dora, I'm me. I probably wouldn't know if a girl liked me even if she came right up and kissed me on the lips."

He blushed as soon as the words were out there.

Dora frowned. "So… do you mind if I…"

On tiptoes, she reached up to kiss him.

It was a soft kiss, gentle, full of warm intention and safety. After a moment, David's hands found her back, more firm and reassuring than she ever could've imagined. And then there were tongues - there are always tongues when you're twenty-five and full of craving, of want - and they were pushing into Dora's front door, struggling to flick the lights on, hearts thumping.

And the rest, as they say, was history.

TWENTY-THREE

After the Gingerbread Restaurant, they continued to walk until Abe's feet were numb with cold and both their noses were bright red and stinging. Neither of them knew when they'd joined hands, but here they were, linked by the touch of their interlocked fingers, warmed by the body heat of the other person. They made their way back across the field, through the archway of lights, walking faster, bolder, now that Abe's elfness was supported and Patrick had taken half the burden.

They crossed the alleyway, crunching over freshly-fallen snow, the sky still reeling from its last shower. There was a breeze in the air, a chill brought about by the wanderings of lonely gusts and weeks of bitter weather, building to the inevitable blizzard. They knew it would be a nightmare to get caught in a storm, to have to hail a cab back to their respective homes, but they didn't want to leave one another – not yet. Although the energy between them was friendly, reserved, saving tender glances and stolen kisses for later… there was a feverish energy in the air between them. No one could deny it.

A hat shop was first, as they ducked out of the cold and into a shop of beanies, woollies, top hats and more, made from lavish North Pole silk and cotton, woven by the elves of the Noël Region. Patrick joked about buying one for Michael, even modelling a flat cap on his older head, but his humour was stilted, raw. So much had changed since they'd once come into shops like these to muck about and have fun, to buy each other gifts and little trinkets, to sneak kisses behind the racks.

So much had changed, dissipated into the air.

The owner was watching them from behind the counter as they made their way round, eyes narrowed. Although Patrick looked dapper in his well-fitting clothes and excellent dress-sense, there was no denying his raggedy mules and rips at the seams of his clothes, patches on his elbows and knees.

Abe had received glances over the last few months because of how thin and withered he'd become, but most people in the local area knew him, respected him. He'd never understood the value in such a fact until now.

"Mr Cane?" the lady chirped, from behind the till. She'd taken off her glasses and hung them around her neck, but was glaring at Patrick with a snooty expression, lips puckered. "Is this man bothering you?"

Patrick turned a petty shade of pink, more with anger than humiliation, but Abe put a hand up before he could say anything.

"He's with me, thank you."

The door chimed as they left.

The street outside was cold, the kind of brittle chill which chips away at fun and rids a day of cheer, of enthusiasm. They were freezing now, huddling beneath not enough layers and battling a fierce wind which threatened to rip them apart. Patrick grabbed Abe's arm again, stealing him down the road and under the canopy of a shop – and then through the open door, and into the warmth.

It was a jewellery shop.

The room was long, stretching on for a good ten metres, but was narrow, awfully so, like most of the stores on Tinsel Street. White stands adorned the walls and hovered freely by the door, gripping to thin air and dripping in necklaces and bracelets and the finest jewels. Dangly pearls; soft amethyst and harsh topaz, glinting in the light; gold, silver and bronze, of all sizes and prices and shades, covering the room from top to toe, extravagant in every sense.

"I bet this place is blooming overpriced," Abe muttered, as Patrick's hand slipped down his arm to meet his fingers, warm and soft as ever, instantly intertwined.

He led him over to a stand on the far side of the room, by the till. There was no one there, but the door had a misty haze around it, a kind of purply spell meant to keep out intruders, thieves, stop customers leaving with items they hadn't paid for.

And on the stand, laid out in boxes and on padded cushions of all different shapes and sizes, were rings.

Big rings, jewelled rings, rings of rose gold and shiny copper, of candy-cane-striped enamel and crystal-clear glass. Rings with little charms, ones with engravings and gems and coins smelted onto the metal, forming intricate patterns of all different types.

"I was going to buy you an engagement ring from here," Patrick said, one eyebrow raised as he skimmed them, first with his eyes, then with his hand. "I… I thought it would've been a nice thought, linking us together forever. That was my plan, you know, when I came to visit you at Santa's Ball that night, when I crashed the party."

Abe was silent, staring down at the rings on the stand,

which gazed back with awful smiles and mocking expressions.

We could've been yours, they chanted, over and over and over, little gemmed faces outstretches. *We could've been yours if you hadn't been so stupid!*

Stupid, stupid, *stupid* –

"I bought one for Michael in the end," Patrick finished, smiling sheepishly and picking at the one on his own finger. It was glossy silver and pattered with little flags, symbolic of the Natale Region. "And Michael came back and bought me a matching one the following year, on our anniversary."

"It's beautiful," Abe said, a little stiffly, and Patrick couldn't hold in the burst of laughter burbling in his throat.

They were silent, then, staring at the rings before them, Patrick still twisting the ring on his wedding finger and frowning down.

Then he said, "Why don't we get matching rings?"

It was a spur-of-the-moment decision, a random idea which suddenly materialised into one which actually made sense. Matching rings, symbolic of their friendship, of their newfound forgiveness, of those weeks they'd spent falling in love all those years ago. Matching rings which weren't declarations of love, necessarily, but were declarations of hope, of happiness, of remembrance.

Matching rings, custom-made by the man at the till, who appeared at the tap of the bell.

"Any specific symbols or names you'd like engraved, Sir?" the man asked, eying Abe and avoiding the scruffy Patrick with a frown. Abe rapped his weathered knuckles against the edge of the till as he thought, finally deciding, without consulting Patrick at all, what their rings must contain, how they must link the two of them together.

"I'd like it to be candy-cane-striped glass," he said, grinning at Patrick as he spoke, never losing his gaze, "symbolic of Abraham Cane. And I'd like to have it engraved with the word *tinsel*."

Patrick was smiling, eyes glossy. The man took down their requests and disappeared into the back to get the ring done, muttering that he'd only be a minute. The pair didn't mind, however, content with browsing the shelves and joking about all the things they'd buy themselves if they were rich, as if Abe wasn't now the very same.

The man came out promptly, clutching a tiny black box in his hand, tied with a ribbon. He waited expectantly for Patrick to examine the goods as Abe dropped coins onto the counter, but the pair kept their box sealed, tucked safely into Patrick's palm.

"Thank you kindly, Sir," he called as they left, still arm in arm, back out into the street.

It was quieter now, fewer Christmas shoppers wandering the warm streets and tucking into mince pies and eggnog, the cobbles bare, stalls already beginning to pack up for the day. They stopped beneath the canopy of a hot chocolate van and stood, where it was warm and dry, to open the box.

Two rings, identical in size and shape and colour and pattern, custom-made for the couple. Candy-cane-striped glass, of red and green and white, the word engraved onto each in fancy black lettering, like a promise. A promise of history, of time and love and truth and commitment, tying them to one another.

Abe took his first, picking up Patrick's hand and sliding it over his podgy finger. The ring was magical, made for them both, and moulded to fit the grooves of his finger as soon as it was on, hooking just above his knuckle.

Patrick took the other, then, lifting Abe's hand in his. It was cold and papery and looked almost worn-through, the veins and bone standing out beneath thin skin as he caressed it, slowly, against his own. The ring was too big, hanging loosely where all flesh had been eaten away, leaving an almost skeleton frame, but it too shrunk and adapted in size and shape to fit Abe's hand.

Just like magic.

"There," Patrick breathed, glancing up to smile. "Perfect."

Next up was the carousel, of course; a risky game, especially at Abe's age and elfness, but Patrick insisted. He poked a finger towards the ride and said, in a low voice, "You want to ride the polar bear?"

Abe winked as he strode towards it on his little wooden walking stick. "Always."

The carousel slowed to a stop, the last riders disembarking, making way for Patrick and Abe. Abe was helped up by an attendant while Patrick chose a pretty reindeer with long lashes and big brown eyes, and they sat back, excited, eager. The carousel started slowly, music low and theatrical, and the two elves had beating hearts and happy, bright expressions as the animals came to life beneath them, all soft, warm flesh and fur you could run your fingers through, great eyes blinking in the bright lights as they moved faster, faster.

Tinsel Street was all a blur, like it had been all those years ago, as Abe looked out through glossy eyes, filled with tears, *tinsel tears*, which burned and ached and hurt, hurt terribly, still hurt now. Shops and Christmas shoppers and little children in fur coats and mittens rode past, laughing, shouting, everything so sickly sweet and warm, like a sugared mince pie, swelling Abe's heart bit by bit by bit.

The ride came to a stop eventually, and Abe found his bearings. On his arm was Patrick, smiling, reassuring. It was almost as though he'd never left.

They began to walk again, Abe's stick clacking against the cobbles, feet weary, body exhausted. They were almost at the end of Tinsel Street now. When Abe noticed the sign above them, he let out a gasp and clapped a hand over his mouth.

They'd come home.

In the merry little land of the North Pole, many regions stretched out in a mismatch of shops and houses and brickwork, each one different in its cultural identity, just like the states of America, stretching out across its plain.

But at its head was the Noël Region. Known best for being home to Santa and all his family, who resided in the palace behind the great, winding drive, the Noël Region was also a land of beauty, and of splendour, and of Christmas cheer. Made entirely from riches and the poverty of others, mind you, but if every elf in the entire North Pole could have even a slice of what Noël had to offer, they'd have gone home happy.

There were cinemas, cinemas selling cinnamon-coated popcorn and ice cream flavoured with brandy, which held mistletoe tied above trees and shared secrets in the breaks. There were stalls lining every street, roasted chestnuts and mulled wine produced in vats, orange juice freshly squeezed, cherries soaked in alcohol and white chocolate stained nutmeg.

And near to the end of Tinsel Street, the quaintest little street in all the land, was the café Abe and Patrick had visited all those years ago, Patrick as a waiter and Abe as a sampler of its infamous candy cane hot chocolate.

It was a little snippet of happiness, tucked between the bins and a pie shop.

There are little cafés like that everywhere, though. The formula isn't unusual. An extensive menu of pretty little coffees and hot chocs, the range of teas far more extensive than builder's and an English Breakfast. Stepping inside was like going back in time, to a place where Christmas was perfectly preserved, kept in a glass jar so as never to fade.

And it's places like that which keep the spirit of Christmas burning bright.

TWENTY-FOUR

"This is where you used to work!" he whispered, shaking his head. "The Wonky Angel. I haven't come back here in years…"

They pushed through the door, bell tinkling overhead and a blast of warm air gushing outwards. Abe was grateful to get out of the cold, for it only made his chest worse, made that awful, hacking cough rise higher in his throat. He led them over to the side of the room to sit by the fire, Patrick letting him sit by the flames with no objection.

The café hadn't changed, really. It still smelt fusty and warm, of cookies and hot chocolate, and the blackboards on each wall spelt out the week's specials in pastel shades, little illustrations of holly and ivy and berries scribbled on each corner. At the front of the room, behind the counter, teens hurried back and forth to finish orders. With those familiar navy aprons tied round their waists, it was almost like going back thirty years.

Abe half expected to see Patrick prance from the backroom wearing his grey hoodie and youthful grin. It only felt like yesterday that he'd stepped through the doors for the first time, allowed Patrick to make him a candy cane hot chocolate and wipe down his table, bustling round the café before they disappeared into the night together.

"So why did you stop working here?" he asked suddenly, turning his head to face Patrick. They were sat opposite one another, knees nudging, on a pair of tartan armchairs. The fire crackled between them, an empty coffee table before it.

"Oh, you know…" Patrick shook his head, as if determined to change the subject, but Abe prodded him to continue. "After the whole outing-myself-on-the-radio thing, they didn't want me working here. It's Tinsel Street; half the customers live in the Noël Region. You never know what people are going to say. The owners didn't want to lose any income. I get it. I *got* it."

Abe blushed, nodding, like he too understood.

But guilt was flooding through his old body, curling through his stomach.

After their little showdown at Santa's Ball, nothing had changed for Abe. More people knew who he was now, so business was pretty good for his dad, but that was all. Abe was a victim; that's what they all thought.

He'd always known it wouldn't be as simple for Patrick. But he'd never truly considered the long-term effects of his actions, how much his life had been altered by it. He'd avoided the café since then, tried his best to find other places in town to take Mollie, until they were engaged and he no longer had to make the effort to take her *anywhere*.

"So I work at the snowball factory full-time now," Patrick finished. "Six days a week, seven till eight."

Abe's eyes opened wide, the guilt swirling faster and faster around his body.

He truly had no idea how lucky he was, did he? Even when he was running the business, he'd barely done a full day's work, leaving the boring jobs to his employees or

Mollie, skipping off to watch European football matches and eat snowballs by the fire. Even on the run-up to Christmas, the most he'd do was a nine till five shift – and even that was rare.

Patrick actually *worked* for his money, grafted all day and night for the lovely clothes he was sprouting, the well-trimmed beard and eyebrows and hair. Abe simply swam in profits, in status and high class and invitations to parties and balls and charity dinners.

He really *was* different to his ex-boyfriend, that was clear.

"Anyway," Patrick said, trying for a smile. "Shall we order?"

They chose hot chocolates, Abe going for a classic candy cane, Patrick debating heavily between salted caramel and strawberry. They arrived in the classic tall glasses covered in cream and pieces of crushed biscuit and candy cane, metal straws stuck out of white mountains of cream, the fancy kind, the kind with a spoon on the one end and a smooth pipe on the other.

"It won't taste as good as mine used to," Patrick joked, taking a sip. "Yep, too much strawberry syrup – I knew it. You always have to go careful on that, or it messes with the chocolate to berry ratio. It's very important."

Abe couldn't help but smile.

They drank their hot chocolates and chatted amiably as the evening progressed, the sky outside growing darker, stormier, rain pelting the windows and shrouding the room in darkness. The candles flickered and customers grew restless and began to leave, throwing up umbrellas and hurtling through the icy rainfall down the street, to where cab drivers sat in the downpour in bedraggled clothing, hoping to return the last few shoppers before heading home.

Abe and Patrick stayed close to the fire with its everlasting flame, dregs of magic from the logs beneath causing it to spit purple, pink and blue sparks. Abe's wizened hands were softer for the heat, his chest looser, body less cramped with pain. The lines on his face weren't so taut and obvious, and his bald head almost shone under the light of a nearby tealight. For the first time since his diagnosis, he felt… free. Relaxed. Like his sell-by date was no longer looming, life no longer a ticking time-bomb.

"So…" Patrick said suddenly, in a low voice. "You never actually told me why you came here, Abraham."

The air between them was less fraught now, smoother, like a gently-flowing river. Patrick's voice wasn't filled with bitterness or anger, more so intrigue and tenderness, the voice of someone simply curious to know an answer.

And Abe… well, he didn't know what to say, not straight away. All sense had flown out of his head the minute Patrick grabbed his hand and held tight, as they'd wandered down Tinsel Street together; a shadow of their former selves.

He breathed heavily now, mind whirring. His head was close to Patrick's – a little *too* close – so close, in fact, that he could make out the individual follicles from which his monobrow had been plucked.

"I needed to apologise," he whispered. "You know I never meant to hurt you, Patrick."

Slowly, Patrick nodded. His hand, now laced with hairs and sporting flat, round fingernails, slid onto Abe's skinny knee. It was soft, light, barely felt through Abe's chinos. The hand slipped further and further, till it was resting just between the top of his legs, where the zip was. He didn't move it from there, but simply made tiny circles with his forefinger, against Abe's leg.

Abe could scarcely breathe, heart pounding as they stayed there, in that position, for another five, ten minutes, time ticking. He swallowed, heart lodged against his oesophagus and brain spinning with feelings, with single thoughts and worries and clear, abject panic –

"I know you didn't," he murmured back, into Abe's ear. "That's what I told everyone. But… you'd left me, Abe. No one believed me."

"And that's why you married Michael…"

"I love Michael. He's a wonderful, wonderful man." Patrick's hand stopped for a second, freezing against Abe's thigh. It was like the whole world had stopped around them, frozen in time, the atmosphere unmoving as their breaths cut through the silence. "But he's not you."

And, slowly, bit by bit, he reached forwards to kiss him.

Abe had shared hundreds – thousands – of kisses with Mollie, but this one, lips hot and urgent and desperate, was something else entirely. Mollie had been soft, sloppy, familiar, a kiss born out of necessity rather than *love*, rather than deep-seated connection. He couldn't remember the last time his lips touched hers.

Kissing Patrick was like returning home after years at war, falling into the pattern of knowing what's *right* and what's *wrong*, slipping back into the routine you needed all along. It felt right, warm and sticky and soft, like caramel, or that same cookie dough feeling he'd given him all those years ago, when they'd first slept together.

Patrick had grown up and matured, just as Abe had grown older, had weathered badly during the storm of life, but their lips, pressed together, hands intertwined, felt just as good as it had done when they were twenty and falling in love for the very first time.

It was wild, all of this was. If you'd have told Abe two weeks ago that he'd be here now, kissing Patrick in the café, eyes watering and heart alive with the fire of love, he wouldn't have let himself believe you.

"You know I could never leave Michael," Patrick said slowly, and Abe nodded, because he knew that, of course. "I don't want this to be an affair, Abe. I want you two to be friends. I just… I need to know what you want, too."

"I only have three months left to live," he whispered hoarsely, as Patrick pulled back to look at him. Sparks were still flying and electricity lit up the air as they stared at one another, eyes locked, hearts pounding loud in the air around them.

A small smile stretched over his ex-boyfriend's face, tugging at the corners of the lips Abe loved so much.

"Then we better make them the best three months of your life."

Patrick met Michael in a bar. It's how so many of these love affairs start, is it not? Patrick was drowning his sorrows over a glass of whiskey, elves bustling around him quietly, politely, without bad intention, when a tap came upon his shoulder and he spun to eye its owner.

It was a man, all ginger hair and smiley face, shorter than him, just, with freckles on his nose and pointed ears red from the cold. He was cute, especially back then, with this warm, wholesome energy Patrick wanted to bottle and tuck inside his coat pocket for later. He was different to Abe, and that was good. Patrick needed difficult. It wouldn't be fair to his future partner if not – or to Patrick.

And so he smiled at the man, tipping his head sidewards as he introduced himself.

Patrick, and Michael.

The names seemed to fit.

Michael was from the Natale Region. He'd grown up in even worse conditions than Patrick, and with something much scarier – an abusive father, who hit him night and day, whose cry made Michael tremble and whose eyes glowed red, even in the sun. He lived in a tiny apartment with his parents and six siblings, all redheads, small and meek and sobbing, always, even when it aggravated their father more. Michael was the eldest, the bravest. He tried to stand up for them, and it almost never ended well.

Michael had had a hard life, and he connected to Patrick on that level. He was working as a cab driver, saving up for his own cab so that he could start his own business, maybe even try to use the radio service to book clients.

But over the years, there always seemed to be something more important than the company, something which stole the hard-earned savings and filtered them away, bit by bit. A leaky roof. The cat they were forced to adopt because it looked like a stray (and it was just too cute). The bars on the window after the robbery.

Money for Dora and David after their third child was born and they could hardly even afford powdered milk from the store.

Living in the North Pole wasn't all glitz and glamour, but one thing Patrick and Michael had was love. They loved each other, had endless fun and laughter, and they loved Patrick's mum, as she was kind and gentle and loved Michael, took him in as one of her own. Michael left home at eighteen and never looked back. He was renting a flat when he met Patrick, and the two quickly decided to merge finances and buy a narrow terrace, right by the factory gates.

They had a long, happy life together, that was for sure. Patrick knew that Michael would be there for him, no matter what, through thick and thin. Michael felt the same. There was always this presence hanging over him, though… Abe. Patrick was Michael's first love, and deep down, Michael knew nothing could compare.

But this isn't an unhappy story. Patrick and Abe might not be perfect, but sometimes, real love never is. We forgive and we forget, and we accept, because we all do bad things, no matter how hard we try to hide it.

Patrick and Abe loved each other like twenty-year-olds do. In a way that's strong and hard and passionate, that hurts, a physical, horrible pain which clings to you like glue. But what Michael had with Patrick… it was real love, raw love.

It was the kind of love that lasts.

TWENTY-FIVE

It was cold outside, and the seat of the wheelchair was hard. Abe's bottom dug into it as the fresh February air spun around him like candyfloss, light and fluffy, yet sharp like ice, grains of sugar grating his skin. It was biting, ridiculously so, and yet he'd tried to wrap up warm to shelter from it, to stop it from progressing his elfness further than he was ready for.

Before him, the ice rink had been decked out for Valentine's Day. It was another holiday the North Pole did surprisingly well; paper hearts, pink and red tinsel, and stalls selling chocolate truffles and individually wrapped roses lined the edge. The rink had made a huge effort to sell tickets, for what they'd dubbed *the most romantic date activity of all time*, and yet the rink was mainly filled with children, scurrying around on their skates and pushing plumped penguins for balance.

In front of Abe, Edward and Sarah were playing on the ice. Sarah was spinning round on her tiny silver skates, a pair she'd begged Lottie and Simon to buy her for Christmas, whirling and twirling and attempting pirouettes. As Abe watched her this time, she swirled so violently that she crashed into a boy, promptly falling flat on her back.

"I'm so sorry!" the boy exclaimed, rushing to help her up.

In his haste, he slipped and fell forwards, right on top of her, face in her puffy pink skirt. "Oh, goodness, I'm *so* sorry –"

"It's okay!" Sarah said, shaking her head and staring at him in wonder. "Er, your hand is on my –"

"Oh!" Flushing, the boy pulled back, so they were sat on the ice opposite each other. They stared for a moment, mouths open in surprise, before the boy said, "I'm Telvin, by the way…"

Beside them, little Edward was trying his very best to leave the side. He kept skating a few centimetres with his hand clutched tight against the barrier, before retracting and clinging to it desperately. His skates had been borrowed from the ice rink and were blue and blocky, far too big for him, but he'd refused the plastic penguin to hold onto – "I'm not a baby, Mum!"

Abe smiled as he watched Edward almost slip over again, clinging in terror to the railing as his feet twisting beneath him. It was wonderful, watching Edward grow up like this, right before his eyes. That was one of the things he hated most about his elfness. One day, the kids would turn into adults without him, starting jobs and getting married and having new lives… and he wouldn't be part of any of it. He wouldn't be at the weddings, the funerals, see them leave school, get jobs in the real world, maybe even go into the pâtisserie business. And that hurt.

He couldn't even wheel the wheelchair himself now, for the strength in his arms wasn't great enough. He simply huddled under a blanket with his hands linked tightly together, watching the rink unfold before him in a mass of squealing and spinning and high-pitched laughter.

Love was high in the air, and it oozed from every inch of the ice. Not just romantic love, of course… but familial love, the love Abe would miss most as he got more and more ill, unable to show those he cared about most how much he was going to miss them. Lottie and Simon were skating as a couple, grinning and giggling as they tried to make their way around, hands held between them and scarfs wrapped determinedly against the cold.

They'd been wonderful, these last few months. Caring and attentive, inviting him round for dinner each night and wheeling him back to his own house later, without a fuss. They'd never pried, overstepped the mark in terms of care, never assuming he couldn't do something or going too far to help him out, doing just the right amount to make his life comfortable. Sometimes, Abe wondered what he'd done to deserve friends like that. And behind them…

Patrick had hold of Michael and was leading him in a slow circle, round the edge of the rink. Michael's thick ginger beard and hair were both hidden beneath bundles of knitwear, blue eyes staring out anxiously at the ice beyond. There was a tiny smile on his partner's face, just readable, as he pulled Michael round and round, tempting him from the edge, clutching his fingers tight, Dora and David mocking them from behind.

In another life, Abe would have felt jealous. Perhaps even a few months ago, his body would have succumbed to violent envy, shaking with pure anger at the sight of Patrick's intimacy with someone else. Michael was fine, of course – kind and funny, if a little awkward – but he wasn't *Abe*, wasn't Patrick's soulmate. Part of him still wanted to keep the brown-eyed gaze all for himself, steal those wide, hairy hands, clutch the newly muscled arms tight against him –

But that was then, and this was now.

Abe knew that Patrick loved Michael. That was pretty

much evident to any onlooker, stranger or not. The way they interacted, touched, spoke… it all screamed *love*. He'd been Patrick's first, and Michael was quite clearly Patrick's last.

He was learning to be okay with that, however hard it may be. The kiss they'd shared in the café had been necessary – it had given closure. Patrick told Michael all about it the minute they returned home, explaining about the elfness and how he only had three months left, how he wanted to spend plenty of time with Abe before he passed, make his last months ones to remember. Michael meant more to Patrick than he could ever explain; one kiss, bridging the gap between heartbreak and redemption, wouldn't change that.

Abe wouldn't have *wanted* it to change things, anyway. He felt guilty enough already. Guilty that he'd broken Patrick's heart all those years ago, humiliated him in front of the nation, made a mess of their once perfect lives. Despite his feelings, he was happy knowing that Patrick was surrounded by love, which was really all he deserved.

And they could still be *friends*. They already were, in a way. That was more than enough for him.

As the whistle went, signalling the end of their hour on the ice, the rink began to empty. Sarah tottered off hand in hand with the boy she'd collided with, flushing as he planted a kiss on the end of her nose before wobbling away in the other direction. She made her way over to Abe with a sheepish grin on her face, and he raised a tired hand to ruffle her hair with equally as big a smile.

Lottie and Simon were next, hyper from the rink and beaming ear to ear. Lottie was pink cheeked and shivering, immediately enveloping Abe in a hug before sitting on the pavement to tug off her skates. Simon went to buy them all a bottled water, which was just so typically *Simon*, and they waited on the benches, all talking at once, until he came back.

"Where are Patrick and Michael?" he queried, turning around to try and spot them. And there they were. Arms around each other and clutching their skates, they wandered towards the party with Dora and David hot on their heels, waving eagerly in their direction.

"Hey!" Patrick said, grinning and shaking hands with Simon. "Hats off to you, Si – you're a blooming good skater!"

They took their seats on the surrounding benches, taking swills from the bottled water and laughing and chatting amiably. It was warm and fuzzy around them, the atmosphere light, friendly. At the end of the day, this was all Abe really wanted. For his friends to get on, and everyone to be *happy*.

"Where to next?" Lottie asked, crouching beside his wheelchair. "We can get food, if you want?"

Thinking hard, Abe glanced round to look at Edward. He was sitting forlornly with his too-big skates still attached to his feet, watching the ice rink as it filled with a new batch of guests. Sarah was still staring at the boy, the one who'd kissed her, as he wobbled back onto the ice with his family. Patrick and Michael still had hold of their skates, and everyone was beaming and hot from the activity, still buzzing with energy.

"How about another round of ice skating?" he suggested, watching as Edward's face lit up and he nodded eagerly.

"Ice skating?" Lottie echoed, frowning. "But aren't you bored, sat here, watching?"

"It's your day out, Abe," Simon echoed. "We can do whatever you want!"

But Abe just smiled. "This," he said, gazing out over the rink, "is *exactly* what I want."

Dear everybody,

If I'm going to die, I might as well tell you all how I really feel before I conk out.

But in all seriousness… thank you. That's all I can say. I haven't always been the best elf I could be in life, and I regret that, I do. I wish I could change things, but I can't, and now, I want to be grateful for what I do have, not what could've been.

And what I do have is family, not by blood, but by friendship, far and wide, the best buddies an elf could ask for. You, Lottie, my best friend, and Simon, a rock, and the kids, little Sarah, the rascal, and Edward, who I adore.

And you, Patrick. My Patrick. You'll always be a friend to me, no matter what. You gave me a lifetime of love, even if you didn't know it. Thank you.

And to my parents, long gone… I'm sorry. I'm sorry you didn't understand me, or even want to try. Maybe it shouldn't be me apologising to you, but the other way round, you heading from the grave to finally say sorry. But you're not here to do that, and I can't live in conflict anymore.

There'll always be so many questions about what I could've done differently, if I could've changed your minds somehow, but there's no point thinking that way now. All I know is that I did love you, somewhere along the way, and probably always will. I can feel you watching over me, and I know you love me too, even if you never had the words to express it.

I don't hate you. I could never hate you.

And if stars can speak to one another, let's talk about it, yeah? Let's try to come to an arrangement. It's never too late.

I'll be seeing you.

All my love,

        Abe x

EPILOGUE

A coffin. Red, of course, like all coffins in the North Pole. Despite it being March, Christmas spirit was still rife in the air, and the funeral parlour Abe had been laid to rest in was no exception.

The room was empty, a coffin laid out on the table in the centre.

The doors opened. There, in suits and ties, sensible black felted mules on each foot, stood the pallbearers. Simon, David, Patrick and Michael… and little Edward, of course, dressed in his own tiny suit and bright purple tie he'd picked from the shop, all by himself. They lined themselves up behind the funeral conductor, who was dressed in his own red suit with its white trim and pointed boots.

Simon took hold of the coffin first, of course, at its front corner, Patrick by his side. They knelt, so that its edges touched their shoulders, as the others filed behind, little Edward at the very back. They lifted the coffin, Abe unsurprisingly light against them, and stood to their full height, Edward on his tiptoes in order to contribute.

The conductor gestured forwards, putting one foot before the other as they followed him, out of the parlour and into the street. It was icy, little to no snow crunching underfoot, the last dregs turned to a thick sheet of slippery sludge beneath them. They were careful not to slip over and drop Abe's body onto the pavement below. The sky was blue, however, despite the dismal weather. The clouds had disappeared, leaving a gently-thawing sun, paying its respects for the late Abraham Cane.

The funeral was to be held just across the street, in the town hall of the Noël Region. It was a spacious room, filled with dark wood panelling and wooden benches.

It was the same town hall, coincidentally, that Abe and Patrick had first met within, all those years ago...

With that, he stomped from the room, crossing the threshold and slamming straight into –

"Ow!"

Abe collided with the snow-ridden pavement, face first, arms and limbs flailing. Ice filled his mouth and slid over his tongue as he choked, turning over into a soft, grey pillow...

"What the..."

He scrambled up, eyes wide staring down at the elf below him.

"I'm so sorry, I didn't mean to –" Abe stopped, heart racing, and took a step backwards. His cheeks were pink and his hands were still trembling.

And there, lying on the pavement, melting the snow beneath him, was the most beautiful boy he'd ever seen...

Patrick swallowed, feeling a lump come to his throat as he passed the very stretch of street they'd had that collision over, Abe pushing into him, throwing him back against the ice. It didn't feel like thirty years since that exchange – it didn't even feel like one – but it was, and so much had happened since then. Looking back at that moment was bittersweet, of course. They'd been so young, so naïve, thinking everything was going to go their way and that they'd be fine, that they'd meet, fall in love, live their happily ever after...

It had taken Patrick every scrap of courage he had to send an initial letter to Abe. To find him out, to track his address, figure out what region he was from, where to send his heart. He'd never expected it to work, for Abe to actually turn up at the café for that hot chocolate.

He hadn't really expected them to fall in love, either. It'd been a nice dream, an ideal, but not something they really thought would *happen*.

But it had.

He'd forever be grateful for that.

The doors to the town hall were open wide as the six elves strode forward, Abe across their shoulders. The benches had been arranged to look like pews, a table in the centre of the hall waiting for the coffin to be placed atop it. It wasn't exactly full, only the first few benches covered in people, but it was full enough. The audience rose in respect as the coffin was carried down the aisle, following the conductor in his fancy red attire, piano spilling classic Christmas carols the whole way.

Abe was placed on the table with a *thud*, little Edward letting his eyes fill with tears as he was led to sit with Lottie and Simon, on the front row. Patrick sat beside them, squeezing Lottie's hand and wrapping an arm round Sarah's throbbing shoulders, as the conductor bowed his head, starting to speak.

"We're gathered here today to celebrate the life of Abraham Cane." He rose his gaze to the level of the audience, expression dull. "A man who no doubt was stolen from us too soon, but who I'm sure we'd all agree lived a full, happy life, a life full of achievements, and who was greatly loved in and around the Noël Region."

Patrick tried to smile as a ripple of agreement ran through

the audience... but he couldn't. The conductor didn't *know* Abe. He didn't understand that his life, while perhaps full of "achievements", hadn't been a happy one – nor had it been lived to the full. Lottie was equally stiff, squeezing his hand as though to say she understood, that he was just repeating the same old spiel, that they knew the real Abe and that that was the only thing that mattered.

"Abraham lived in this area his whole life," the conductor continued. "It was where he grew up, met his best friend, Lottie, and went to school, where he excelled. It was where his parents had their shop, until they sadly passed, leaving the business solely to Abraham. The business was his passion, and it too flourished until Abraham made the decision to sell it, following the death of his beloved wife and soulmate, whom he also met in this area... the lovely Mollie –"

That was it – Patrick couldn't take it anymore.

He stood, fists shaking in fury, and made his way over to the conductor, who looked confused. Politely but firmly, he grabbed the piece of paper from his hand and – in three deft, quick strokes – tore it to shreds, dropping them to the ground so that they fell like confetti.

"Excuse me," the conductor said, blinking and attempting to pick up the pieces, clearly flustered. "Could you –"

"Leave the speech to me."

With that, the conductor let out a little huff, shuffling back to let Patrick take centre stage.

This was it. This was his chance. His chance to set the record straight, tell everyone the truth about Abe, the truth he'd spent his whole life trying to conceal...

He opened his mouth, ready to speak, but something stopped him. Gazing out over the audience, thirty or so people who'd known Abe, who'd loved him, who'd respected him…. he just couldn't do it.

There was nothing wrong with being gay. Abe shouldn't have had to hide it for so long, keep it under wraps, marry Mollie, close his eyes to all the wonders of the world he could've been experiencing.

Patrick knew that.

Deep down, Abe had known that, too.

But the rest of the Noël Region… they didn't know that, would never really *understand*.

On the back row, sat nearest to the aisle, were Abe's elderly neighbours. They were a traditional pair, sat with an elf he assumed to be their grown-up son. Maybe they wouldn't care if they knew Abe's true identity; maybe they would. That was just it. Patrick didn't know. But wasn't his place to tell.

Beside them, Abe's old schoolteacher perched. She was in a rush to leave, was just staying for the speeches and any eulogies there might happen to be, and desperately needed to get back to the school, where she still worked, almost forty years after she'd begun. She'd always found Abe to be a quiet child, but an interesting one, surprisingly smart and contemplative. She liked him. He interested her.

And Abe liked her, too.

On the middle row, three old women sat, pointed ears peaking from a bed of tightly-permed curls. They'd been customers of Abe's parents, back in the day, and later customers of Abe himself, handing over their old shoes at the end of each year to send to deserving children across the globe. They'd always liked Abe, and had taken a special shine to Mollie. They'd been devastated when they found out the couple couldn't have children. They loved Abe, loved him like the son none of them had.

But again – it wasn't Patrick's place to tell them who Abe really loved.

It had been Abe's. Abe made the choice to keep his identity a secret, and as much as Patrick wished he hadn't, he respected that. He understood.

Because, as Patrick stood there, watching over the audience, realisation was dawning. Times were changing. The younger generation, the one he and Abe were a part of, weren't the problem – and neither was the older. They didn't understand it, didn't think it was right, *normal*, because of the world they were brought up in, what they were told, taught.

Exposing Abe's sexuality to all the people who loved him wouldn't change their negative views, wouldn't help the North Pole become a more accepting place.

If Abe had wanted that, wanted any of it, he would have done it in his own time.

The memory of Abraham Cane as a kind, decent man, a good businessowner and husband, a great citizen of the Noël Region... and as a great friend.

Being gay had nothing to do with it.

It was just who he was.

"Abraham Cane," he began, staring out at the audience with a clear smile and wide eyes, "was a great friend of mine. I've known him since I was twenty, and I can assure you he was one of the very best..."

***

After the funeral, a short get-together was held at the Gingerbread Restaurant. Everyone from the service went, including a collection of Abe's old school friends, and colleagues he'd known whilst working in the shop, neighbours he'd met both at his old flat and in his current house. The restaurant had been decked out in classy silver tinsel and bunting, simple sandwiches on each table, sour cream snowballs in bowls around the room, confetti sprinkled everywhere. It truly was a celebration of Abraham Cane, of his life and those who loved him, of his presence as part of the Noël Region.

There were a lot more people turning up now, more than they'd even anticipated, and the room was filling up fast; they'd long lost count of how many extra chairs they needed. The kitchen was working overtime to keep up with the sandwich supply, and the decorations were soon lost amid a sea of people, the surrounding area too full to even spot who was standing next to you, let alone move.

But on a table by the door, huddled together with a round of candy cane hot chocolates – not as good as the ones from the café, of course – were Patrick, Lottie, Simon, Edward and Sarah. Michael had disappeared off with Dora and David, leaving them to have some time to themselves, time to grieve, to celebrate Abe. The room was loud, people bustling about and catching up, but their table was quiet in its sadness, heads bowed over mountains of whipped cream.

"Abe would've loved this." Lottie spoke eventually, breaking the silence. She licked up some of the cream just for something to do, mint sauce stinging her tongue. "The food, the decorations… everyone here, together."

Patrick nodded, shivering. He couldn't deny that this was right up Abe's street; Simon and Lottie had done a great job organising it all, putting the whole thing together. He took a sip of his own drink, but it tasted too minty, the flavour too harsh against the chocolatey goodness. He still made the best hot chocolates in the North Pole – that was a fact.

"It's wonderful how many people have turned up, too…" Simon contemplated. "Come on, kids, drink up!"

But the children were near tears, Edward's mouth trembling and Sarah's eyes glittering.

"We're not thirsty."

Simon rolled his eyes, holding up his mug. "Would Uncle Abe want you to be sad?"

One at a time, they shook their heads solemnly. Simon nodded his agreement, jerking his mug about so that the drink splashed over the sides a little, wetting the silvery tablecloth.

"A toast," he said, holding it firm. "To Abraham Cane, our best friend and brother."

Through glittering eyes, Lottie and Patrick raised their own mugs. The children did the same, using two hands to keep the huge vats of hot chocolate afloat in the air, as they pushed them forwards in unison, clinking together in the centre of the table, cream and chocolate and dark green mint sauce gushing all over the table and dripping off the edge.

"To Abraham Cane."

To Abraham Cane.

COOKING WITH PATRICK!!
how to make candy cane hot choc:

INGREDIENTS:

50g dark chocolate
1pt semi-skimmed milk
2 scoops vanilla ice cream
x2 finely chopped candy canes
1tsp peppermint extract

HOW TO MAKE:
1. Firstly, you're going to stir the chopped dark choc into your milk in a pan on medium heat - not to boil it, but to warm it through.
2. Add the peppermint extract and most of the candy cane chunks, stirring well.
3. Next: prepare your mugs!
4. You'll need two mugs, and a few spoonfuls of milk in a shallow dish, and the remaining candy cane chunks in a separate dish.
5. Turning the mugs over, dip the rims into your milk until they're wet. Then dip the rims into candy cane chunks until they're well coated.
6. Pop a scoop of ice cream into each mug, and pour the hot chocolate over the top to fill.
7. You can even put a candy cane in each mug to use as a stirrer, and add whipped cream.
8. Drink while still hot!

COOKING WITH PATRICK!!
how to make mince pie mocktails:

INGREDIENTS:
500ml grape juice
500ml cranberry juice
1 cinnamon stick
3 cloves
1 thinly sliced orange
2tbsp honey
2tbsp sugar

HOW TO MAKE:
1. Pour the juices into a pan, leaving a few tablespoons in a shallow dish. Add the spices, and simmer for ten minutes.
2. Stir in your honey until dissolved, and add the slices of orange. Remove the spices to serve.
3. You'll need several mugs - I'd use heat-proof glasses, but you can use regular mugs or even paper cups!
4. Bring back the juice you placed in a shallow dish, and put the sugar in a separate dish.
5. Turning the mugs over, dip the rims into your juice until they're wet. Then dip the rims into sugar until they're well coated.
6. Pour the mocktail into the mugs, distributing the orange slices evenly. Enjoy!

GETTING FESTIVE WITH ABE
a couple's xmas bucket list:

- My favourite festive thing to do at christmastime is to go for a winter walk. It doesn't have to be super snowy or festive, but wrap up warm and enjoy the chilly
- air.
- Decorating a gingerbread house or men is a really cute way to spend a cold evening together. You can buy kits from the shop or try to make your own, and decorate them using tubes of traditional white icing. You could even try to make gingerbread lookalikes for you and your partner!
- Create a christmas movie bucket list. This could be movies from your childhood or newer ones... and both of you can rate each out of five.
- Make christmas cards together. This is a really fun activity and you can do it in so many ways... by using potato halves to stamp white paint onto a brown card and make a snowman, or cutting snowflakes from white paper to cover black card.
- You could even make and write a romantic christmas card for each other, and do an exchange!

- Making Christmas baubles together is a quick way to ensure your relationship lasts. If this is your first Christmas together, you could make a bauble to commemorate your first December as a couple, and promise to put it on your shared tree one day. Use glitter glue to write on a gold bauble - or whatever you want!
- Make salt dough decorations! Salt dough is a super cheap, easy dough which can last for years, and is so fun to make and decorate. Find a recipe online, shape the dough in any fun way, bake it, and decorate with paint and a good sealant. You could gift them to each other.
- Have a Christmas dinner together - especially if you don't spend the big day with each other. Make a big roast and mocktails and watch movies, and exchange stocking filler gifts! I would have loved to do this.

And if you don't have a partner to spend the festive season with, don't fret. You can do all of these activities by yourself, or with your friends, or with an aunt or your nan or a group of classmates. Christmas can be a lonely time, but it doesn't have to be. Make plans, and do Christmas your way! Have fun x

acknowledgements

I wrote 'Tinsel Tears' when I was in sixth form, just seventeen years old, at the end of 2020. My only intention was to write a story of happiness and true love, a book which would uplift people, make them smile. I wanted it to be wholesome and festive, because that's the best thing about Christmas! It didn't need to be dark or sad or political (because my version of the North Pole is entirely... well, fictional). And now, three years later, I wanted to publish the expanded edition and spread some lovely Christmas joy with the world.

First and foremost, thank you to everyone at sixth form who inspired this book in some way or other, and for your never ending love and laughs and support. I remember doing little doodles in my exercise book and writing pages and pages of this book after school, and being so overwhelmed with Christmas cheer and that teenager-y love you're so desperate to put into words. This is the first book I've written (and published) not set in Yorkshire, but there's something so warm and wholesome and lovely about its essence, that it almost feels like it could be.

Thank you to my first readers, as always... and to Christina, first and foremost, for telling me over and over that it was one of your favourite books, for helping me to see the wonder in 'Tinsel Tears' for what it really is. Thank you to the lovely reader from somewhere far across the world, for telling me how much my story opened your eyes up to different kinds of love when you first read it on Wattpad. I've changed a lot since that moment – and so has this book, initially only 40,000 words long and full of plot holes – but I still recall exactly how it felt to hear that my words had helped someone, in some way, and helped them become, in their words, a better person.

And to Sana, forever my confidante, one of only two people I told about the release of this book, before I surprised the rest of the world. To Will, for your hard work on this book, as well as everything else.

Thank you to everyone in my real life who helped forge the image of Christmas I keep so closely to my heart now. The family members who gift handmade presents in jars and tissue paper, and my parents, for decorating the tree with baubles we made at five, seven, out of salt dough and felt. Thank you to both my primary and secondary schools, for the Christmas tunes and quizzes and heads-down-thumbs-up marathons on the last day of term. That's what Christmas truly means to me.

And thank you to you, my readers, to all of the people who've read and supported my books across the world, whether by choice or because it was free on your Kindle, available in your library or charity shop. I'm not a romance writer by any means, and I love that you all eat up any book I write, no matter the genre.

It still astounds me that I get to do this without concern, that I can publish my books and someone, somewhere, whoever you are, will want to buy and read.

That will never not mean the world to me.

NOBODY KNOWS...

GUIDED

BOOK ONE

EMMA SMITH

NOBODY KNOWS WHAT HAPPENED THAT NIGHT... NOBODY BUT MACEY.

NORMAL, RIGHT?

MIDNIGHT SHERBET

EMMA SMITH

YOUNG LOVE NEVER LASTS...
BUT FRIENDSHIP MEANS FOREVER.

EMMA SMITH

is a young adult author from Yorkshire, England. She wrote and illustrated her first "book" when she was seven years old and hasn't stopped writing since. When she's not walking on the beach or drinking an iced coffee with a crumpet and some chocolate, you'll probably find her reading something dark and mysterious… and most certainly YA.

@themmasmith on Instagram

emmasmithbooks.com

Printed in Great Britain
by Amazon